# THE MAMMOTH QUEST:

## AN EPIC EXPEDITION INTO THE PAST

### BY

### CALVIN SMITH

RoseDog 🐾 Books

PITTSBURGH, PENNSYLVANIA 15238

RoseDog Books
585 Alpha Drive, Suite 103
Pittsburgh, PA 15238
Visit our website at www.rosedogbookstore.com

ISBN: 978-1-6461-0356-0
eISBN: 978-1-6461-0402-4

# CONTENTS

For my
Mother and Dad, Wife and Daughter,
Grandson and Granddaughter and the many
relatives, friends, teachers, colleagues and students
who taught and encouraged me through
the many years of exploration and discovery

# Author's Preface

All of the dates, activities, tools and customs are based on the evidence acquired from the archaeological record of the Clovis and Folsom Periods beginning in the 1920's when investigations at the Folsom Type Site in northern New Mexico revealed that humans had indeed killed giant, extinct bison with what became known as Folsom Points, making them contemporaneous with Pleistocene animals in the Americas. In the 1930's the Clovis Type Site was excavated at Blackwater Draw, New Mexico which became the first confirmed mammoth kill site where artifacts were found *in situ* imbedded within the bone bed including what were to become known as Clovis points. All of the research, excavations and analysis help determine who these people were, when they got here, why they selected these sites, what artifacts they used to kill and butcher the megafauna they encountered and how they survived the changing environments and predators they faced.

# Part I

# Chapter 1

# Introduction

**A** crisply dressed young man is making his way up a driveway to a large Hogan – at least 16' on each of the 8 sides – it is cold – snow on the ground and he doesn't have a coat. It is late January and in Colorado west of Colorado Springs. He rings the doorbell – a gruff voice answers – "I'm coming, I'm coming" – Dr. Robert Roby, a white bearded man in his late 60's but in good shape answers the door. "What do you want boy? I'm retired and I don't want to talk to anyone. I'm writing two books and one of them is two volumes".

I know sir – uh, Dr. Roby, I'm here from NASA and would like to talk to you about translocation – teleportation specifically.

What the ..... ?

You may have heard of our efforts to take researchers back in time since our space programs have been scrubbed. We know you have written about the need to actually see and be with the Clovis people.

Geeze! What do you know about – how did you know – about that?

Well Sir – may I come in?

Sure come on in – what the hell are you doing here without a coat?

Well sir, it was 75 degrees when I left Houston and it was supposed to be in the 40's here today and I...

Never mind – do you want some coffee?

No sir, but I will take some tea.

Under his breath, damn pansies – don't even drink coffee anymore.

3

Sir?

Never mind I'll nuke some H2O and my wife has all kinds of tea – what would you like?

Just regular Lipton would be great.

Under his breath, Geezze! The boy is 180 degrees off center.

Sir?

Never mind, it'll be ready in a minute.

Thanks.

Would you like something with it?

Cream & sugar if you have it sir.

I'll get it and quit calling me sir.

Yes sir, I mean Dr.

They sit down at an old oak table with one leg propped up with a block of wood where one of the wheels has broken off.

Now what's this about? Yes, I have said I would like to go back in time to observe the Clovis people – but how would all of this work?

Well sir...

Rob wags his finger.

You see Dr. Roby the teleportation process takes you back to an exact time and place and you have exactly a year to get back to the exact spot where we drop you off in order to pick you up, but if you miss the first opportunity you have only one more chance to return exactly one year later if you don't make it the first time otherwise you will be caught in that time period.

Whoa, wait a minute, you're telling me that you now have the capability to transport someone back in time AND retrieve them?

Yes sir.

Geeze! I had no idea this would actually ever happen, especially in my lifetime. I knew IBM and GE and the Japanese were working on it but they aren't there yet...are they?

Well Dr., I'm not sure how far along they are but we, NASA has had some success and the next window of correlation is back to the interval that you are interested in.

And why did you pick an old man like me?

Well Dr. I'm not the one to ask that question you would have to go up to the next administrative level.

4

This is exciting news but…I don't know…when would all this happen IF I even consider it?

May 11<sup>th</sup> is our next window of opportunity.

Geeze, that's not long.

That's why I'm here Dr. I, we have a plane at the airport to fly you to NASA. You mean right now?

Well as soon as you are ready. We'll wait as long as necessary.

A strikingly beautiful 60's woman with naturally grayish white hair enters the house carrying groceries.

Della, this is, uh……what was your name again?

Bruce Ferguson, 'mam, very pleased to meet you.

And what brings you to our home?

Rob gives Ferguson a stern look and shakes his head slightly but most negatively.

I'm here to ask Dr. Roby about his work on Paleo Indians.

And what would be your background to have this interest?

My PhD is in anthropology 'mam.

The gentleman was just leaving Della.

Nice to meet you 'mam.

And likewise, I'm sure.

Rob and Ferguson walked out to his car.

I can't make a commitment yet. I have a LOT of questions AND a lot of explaining to do to Della AND get her approval IF I decide to accept the offer.

That's alright Dr. – take as long as you need – here is my card just call me on my cell when you are ready – uh, make a decision.

Oh, by the way please do not mention this to anyone else at this point.

OK…sure, anyone in their right mind would think I'm crazy anyway.

It was snowing again so Rob goes over and closes the back window on his pickup shell. He really didn't want to face Della about any of this but knows he must and goes back into the house.

Now! What was that all about **Dr.** Roby?

Well, he's actually from NASA and because they have been cut back on their space travel they have been working on translocation or more accurately, teleportation.

And what does that have to do with you?

Well, they want me to go back…

Back to where, when – how?

Well, I'm not sure how yet, but they want to fly me to Houston to get the details but the when is May 11<sup>th</sup>.

And how far back?

Well as you are well aware my expertise is Paleo, Clovis specifically, so I'll have to figure the most accurate time I can intercept them.

And how long would you be gone?

A year.

A year!

Yeah, they would pick me up exactly a year later at the same spot...

This is insane – what if ...**what if!**

Della, you know this is the chance of a lifetime, I don't know why but they are offering it to me!

Crazy damn fool! What about me? AND Nita!

I would work out some help and insurance and...

**STOP** right there! You **KNOW** that's not the point – what if you don't make it back – I know from your talks about sabertooths, giant bears and humongous lions...

I know, I know, but I think I can take care of myself and make it back OK.

**OK** is not good enough – I don't like any of this, it's too risky – they may not, probably don't know if this is going to work – you are almost 70 years old and need a new knee and a shoulder repair and May the 11<sup>th</sup> is not enough time to get that done and do the rehab. What the hell are you thinking? Taking a chance like this?

Well at least I should fly down there and get some more details...

Details! What else do you need to know? That's enough I'm not talking to you anymore.

Rob, to himself – Well, that didn't go very well.

Silence through dinner and into bed.

As they were lying in bed – I know this is your passion and I married you 40 odd, very odd, years ago accepting your peculiarities – you might as well go see what this is all about. BUT you better damn well come back with some major explanations AND you are going to call Nita!

Yes 'mam – I'll call Ferguson in the morning – they've got the plane waiting at the airport.

Great! What else don't I know?

Nothing dear – only the 2 year part.

What did you say?

Nothing dear, good night and thank you…for your understanding.

SURE!

Next morning – Mr. Ferguson it looks like I'll be going with you. What time do you want to leave?"

At your convenience sir, uh, Dr.

I'm about an hour away from the airport.

Come to the private entrance and identify yourself – I'll be waiting.

I've never been to the private entrance, where is it?

The far northeast corner. You will see some signage.

Rob as he parks under the covered parking, "If they are asking me to do this they are going to pay for it".

He makes his way to the private entrance and rings a bell at an iron gate. A uniformed TSA officer comes to greet him – "Are you Dr. Roby?"

Yes.

We've been expecting you, may I see a photo ID – either a passport or current driver's license.

Rob finally gets his driver's license out of his billfold.

Quite alright sir – and the gate swings open. As Rob turns the corner there is Ferguson, same coat and tie, waiting.

Really glad you are coming Dr.

And why is that Mr. Ferguson?

Well sir you were the #1 choice and we are running out of time to get you ready.

Whoa, wait a minute, before we get on that plane I want it to be perfectly clear that I have NOT agreed to anything – that will be a decision my wife and I will make when I get back.

Yes sir, I understand sir, we are just pleased you will consider it.

Whatever, which plane is it?

This way sir, uh, sorry, Dr.

It was a Gulfstream – big – fancy – shiny, freshly washed.

NASA lets you fly this around to pick up old wore out archaeologists?

No sir, it is a private plane with its own pilots. I've never flown in anything like this or even been in one until now.

Private?

Yes sir, we have a major patron for the project or we wouldn't be able to pull it off.

And who is it?

I'm sorry Dr. I'm not at liberty to say.

Whatever.

They board and are welcomed by a beautiful stewardess – May I take your bag sir?

No 'mam, I may do some writing on the way.

Yes sir, just stow it under your seat until we are in the air.

Yes 'mam.

A young red headed man, slightly balding comes back and introduces himself as Captain O'Malley and welcomes him aboard. "The flight will be quick 2 ½ hours and we'll be landing at the NASA field".

Rob sat next to the window Ferguson sat in the aisle seat across from him. To make small talk he asked him what his dissertation was on.

Native Americans, "The initial contact between the French and English on the Northern Plains and how that set the stage for future encounters".

Well, I guess that's a long enough title – did you ever consider the initial, first contact between the Spanish and the Indigenous peoples 200 years earlier?

Yes, but there had already been a lot done and published on that period.

Yep, I guess so – the stewardess brings out a platter of snacks. Rob takes some peanuts and asks for an honest, non-diet, Dr Pepper.

So they settle back and as the plane takes off, Rob goes into a long introspection of "what if's": What if, the 30-40 year pluses or minuses in the Carbon dating are during the time he gets there. What if, he never sees anyone else – the population was scattered and limited as far as they knew and what if he gets injured or killed – most primitive societies do not appreciate or accept outsiders. They are considered an immediate threat to territory and their established culture. What if he loses the place they drop him – he has got to mark it well and make sure he gets back in exactly a year...

What is he going to take with him – GPS for sure – but that's crazy, there would be no satellites! And a laptop or iPad would not be rechargeable – so pencils & waterproof journals – a weapon – but what kind? – Big enough to kill a bear bigger that a Kodiak or polar. Geeze! – I'm getting loaded down already – plus my sleeping bag & extra clothes, boots and water purification system…I've got to think a lot more about this. Ferguson was texting most of the way so there was very little conversation.

The stewardess reappears, "We will be arriving in about 6 minutes, please buckle up and put your seat backs in their upright positions".

The landing was the smoothest Rob had ever experienced.

Ferguson was first out and was waiting at the bottom of the ramp to introduce him to a Colonel Mathis and General Woodward.

Rob, to himself – A GENERAL! Geeze, I didn't expect a General – maybe this is a pretty big deal.

The General welcomes Dr. Roby, "We are pleased to have you here, let's go sit down a while and discuss this proposal".

They all get in an older Lincoln limo and went into the heart of NASA – The office was palatial but a little worn, certainly from the good years.

We have a breakfast or maybe more of a brunch buffet over here – Ferguson was already going through followed by the Colonel.

The General was much more courteous allowing Rob to go before him – it was a great spread – bacon, eggs, ham, sausage, pancakes, waffles, toast, muffins, apple and orange juice, coffee and tea, for Ferguson of course.

Small talk about families and careers follows throughout the meal but then the General says, "Are you serious about this?"

Well, I guess it is a dream of every Paleo Indian archaeologist – what did they look like? What were their basic cultural traditions? What were their daily means of survival? What were their burial practices? It is – would be an honor to represent my colleagues as the first to accomplish this challenge.

Now I have a question – why me?

The Colonel finally chimes in. "You have been very vocal about wanting to go back in time but of all the qualified professionals we surveyed you were the only one who has hunted all his life, we wanted someone to be able to survive and even at your age it looks like you have the best chance".

The General responds, "Actually, you are the best choice to carry this off and we want to do everything within our abilities to encourage you to accept the endeavor".

Well, as I told Mr. Ferguson this will have to be a decision between my wife and me.

Of course – we want to offer you a $120,000 annual salary for life which your wife will receive as $10,000 a month, tax free, even if you don't return and we will put her up at the Broadmoor during your absence – or until her death or decision to relocate.

The Colonel finally breaks the long silence, "There are some considerations you need to be aware of that may have an impact on the translocation – we will have to remove the three teeth that have fillings".

Whoa! How did you know I had three fillings? – Never mind I don't want to know – But why?

Well, if you have tooth problems you won't have access to treatment. But, primarily, everything that is not flesh is non-transferable.

Wait a minute! You're telling me that I'm going back buck naked?

Well, yes, that's the bottom line – no pun intended.

Another long silence with Rob rubbing his beard and forehead.

Wow! I wasn't ready for that one! I had planned on – never mind – I really have to consider – I'll really have to think long and hard about going back without protection and clothing necessary to survive.

The General then says, "That's why we've brought in three of your colleagues to help you plan your arrival and survival".

Who?

Well there is Harry Ross, the Paleoecologist, Bill Leftwich the Paleo-anthropologist and Mike Anderson, who you've collaborated with on some geoarchaeology papers.

I know Harry and of course Mike and have read Bill's work but why him?

The Colonel offers, "He has done a lot of work on burials and interpreting what is known about prehistoric populations".

Yeah but…

The General responds, "It will be clear tomorrow – or at least more relatable, we are bringing them in the morning – but right now we want you to see and understand the process – the Colonel and the Ferguson will take you over to the Center – I'm afraid I have other commitments – but whatever your decision thank you for coming".

Well it has been interesting General.

This whole endeavor has been interesting Dr. Roby, I'll see you later.

The "Center" was a circular peaked domed structure and was the only new looking building what with the salt air combined with the pollution of Houston and the numerous refineries in the immediate vicinity things start to get an obvious patina very quickly. On entering however, it was sparse – IKEA like, with what appeared to be an outer personnel and possible public area encircling the immediate interior with offices, conference rooms, cafeteria, gym and even a small swimming pool – one of those with forced water flow. Rob was led into the next level that looked like the scenes from all the space scuttle films and the live TV reporting. Everything within the inner circle looked in on a clear space with a large circular object with a hole in the middle extending downward almost to the floor.

Two individuals in lab coats approach and were introduced as Dr. David Baker a physician and Dr. Robert Ellis a physicist and project Director.

Dr. Ellis – "Just call me Bob"

Dr. Baker – "Good to meet you Dr."

Rob – "Likewise gentlemen"

Bob suggests they go into the conference room.

David asks if he would like some coffee or tea or a coke?

An honest Dr Pepper please

You bet. Something for you Ferguson?

No thanks, I'm fine.

Bob begins, "We'll try to be brief, but thorough Dr. and answer any questions you might have. The process of teleportation/translocation has been on paper a good while and became implanted in popular culture, especially during the Star Trek "Trilogy", as he motions the quotes with his fingers, and has actually been in place here for several years".

In place?

Yes we started with chimps transporting them to another locality here at NASA in the same time continuum and then back here – they were heavily sedated at first to limit their movements in and out of the designated space requirements but that worked well so we started with time warps going back a little further – only a month at first, selecting them from our resident population placing them and then taking them at night so no one would notice and that also worked.

So only a month in a confined space?

Yes, but then we did one for a year, we told our keepers that they would see an added chimp for a period of time and that we would control its arrival and departure and not to worry if it wasn't there some morning but to make sure it was in its enclosure every night and that was successful.

But we're talking 13,000 years ago for the Paleo period.

Yes, we know, but we have identified a very dependable correlation cycle and have tested the possible results and all of our calibrations are accurate. We wouldn't proceed unless we knew that we could get you to a date and retrieve you exactly a year later.

Or two?

Yes, those are our only positives – we may be able to go out 3-5 years in the future with the experience gained from these first trials but we lose accuracy as the deferential gets greater.

Trials!

Yes, you are THE pioneer in this first attempt to go back that far but I, we, are very confident all systems are a "go".

But you can't track me and you can't come and get me at a different location?

No sir.

And there is no means of communication or emergency retrieval?

No sir.

David butts in, "That's why we are bringing in your colleagues to help you think and explore all the probable outcomes and challenges to give you the best opportunities for observation and survival".

WOW! And I'll be going buck naked!

Yes, but you will have a great advantage over any other 70 year old – ever.

Why do you say that?

Well, every foreign particle, every grain of sand or dust that is in your lungs will be left behind – as well as the wire in your jaw –

Geeze! You know about the wreck I was in in the 1980's? Well, of course you do!

Yes, but also we believe your whole body will be rejuvenated to some degree by the experience.

Well, at least now I know why my teeth have to come out.

Yes sir, but we'll give you a lifetime dental and medical to replace those teeth – as well as any other needs that may occur.

I can't complain about what you are offering – but all of this must be OKed by wife.

Bob then interjects, "We understand, but are YOU ready?"

I'm not sure yet – my colleagues may have some things I haven't considered or some disadvantages of going in naked to an environment full of things wanting to eat me – either one may sway the decision.

12

For now let's get you back to the General for today's wrap up – It's been good meeting you "Dr. Rob".

Likewise "Dr. Bob" – and you "Dr. David".

On the way back Rob asks Ferguson – "You haven't had much to say David".

No sir, Dr. – I'm just here to assist you with anything you need or in anyway I can to make your visit productive.

Understood – let me ask you a question.

OK.

Since your dissertation makes you THE expert on the Native American contact period – on the Northern Plains that is – what would be your thoughts on red headed occupants already residing in North America as the Siberians entered the same space?

It comes down to population dynamics – it may have been a few Siberians passing through and accepted at first but as more came the Redheads would become defensive and as the Siberian population increased there would be conflicts with the greater numbers prevailing.

Makes sense – would the survivors be assimilated?

Not likely – I found none of that – voluntarily anyway – as slaves of course – thus the dominant population remained relatively pure. What was interesting was the tribal units remained stable even with the influx of Anglo–Europeans well into the 19th century.

You have confirmed my thoughts and I appreciate your evaluation of one of the many questions we have about the Paleo period – and one of my reasons for wanting to go back.

Back at the General's office he asks, "How was your visit to the Complex?"

Most revealing and the questions keep getting more numerous.

I understand. I want you to know we have not spoken to your colleagues except to tell them we needed their input on the possibility of someone to be translocated back to the Paleo Period.

They don't know I've been selected?

Not until tomorrow morning when you meet with them. I will be there to introduce you as our choice and leave but none of our people will be present during your conversations.

That's a laudable approach and I appreciate your thoughtfulness in the arrangements.

We are grateful for your openness to consider this most unique prospect.

Well, it had been just a dream – until now –

I would like Ferguson to take you over to our guest quarters where you can order from our 5 star menu including some real Texas barbeque or some Cajun crawfish ettouffe or both and visit with your wife on our phone.

Yep, I need to do that – both.

It's been a pleasure Rob.

Me too General – they shake hands.

At the guest quarters Rob ordered both barbeque and the crawfish and called Della.

Well it's been one a hell of a day...

Tell me about it.

Well I've met with a Colonel, a General, a physicist and a physician and finally got something out of Ferguson.

Wow! That's pretty highfalutin' company. Well tell me what happened.

I met with the General & Colonel first – they are very well informed and committed to the project and selected me from the entire field.

Why?

Well because of my expertise and I've hunted all my life.

Well that's an interesting juxtaposition.

What may interest you is $10,000 a month during my expedition – tax free!

Wow!

And something else that may interest you. They will put you up in the Broadmoor while I'm gone.

You're kidding – they didn't really say that?

Yep.

I'm floored – I don't know what to say – but you are right – I am becoming more interested. That could be the security we need for our retirement.

Yep.

But I've kind of gotten used to your oddities. Have you decided what you are going to do?

Not yet, I'm meeting with Harry and Mike and Bill Leftwich in the morning to explore the pluses and minuses – that – they will help.

Well I know this has been your dream for years and after a lot of thought about all the possibilities I want it to be your decision – I will live with it either way – but you may not!

I know – but with us looking objectively at challenges tomorrow I can better evaluate the opportunity.

Della – I trust your judgment – I love you and will support your decision. Pause – and you know my favorite place is the Broadmoor.

Yes I know! And I love you too.

The next morning Ferguson picks up Rob and hurries to the General's office – it is exactly 8AM when they enter. Bill, Harry & Mike were already there helping themselves to the buffet – the General is standing behind his desk drinking his coffee.

# Chapter 2

# Decisions

**D**r. I've told these gentlemen that you have been selected to be the first to go back through our teleportation program and they seem pleased. I've also told them that you have to be back to the drop site exactly a year later with no more than a second year leeway.

Mike greets Rob, "Hello Rob, it's been good knowing you – and thanks for the honorarium."

Hello Mike, thanks for the moral booster. Hello Harry, good to see you again. Hello Bill, finally good to shake hands.

Likewise – looking forward to the visit.

Harry asks, "What the hell makes you think you can pull this off?"

The General interrupts, "With that gentleman, I think Ferguson and I will leave you to various discussions about which we need not be involved."

Everyone thanks the General for his consideration and courtesies and the General and Ferguson leave.

In answer to your question Harry – I don't know if I can – I'm not sure if anyone can.

Mike asks, "Did they tell you why they picked you?"

Rob answers as he starts serving his plate, "Yeah, they said it was because I said in print I wanted to be the first to go back AND that I was a life long hunter AND that I was in good shape."

Harry adds, "Makes sense – You are the only one of us who hunts – so you know game animals – what kind of weapon are you taking?"

None

Mike exclaims, "What!?"

No, this process can only transport flesh and bone so I would be going back buck naked.

Harry – Geezee! – This gets crazier by the minute!

Tell me about it – that's why I need you to help me think this through – I haven't made up my mind yet.

Mike submits, "You will be facing an environment we can only speculate about but we do know there were lots of very big predators that probably thought humans were pretty tasty."

I know.

Harry asks, "If you are serious about this when would you go?"

The 11th of May.

Bill warns, "That's not long enough to get ready."

Mike responds, "What do you mean?"

Let me give you just one example. Rob, when was the last time you went barefooted?

Well – I don't remember...I guess when we took Nita to the beach.

Well that's nice soft sand, you are going to have to toughen up your feet or you are going to be crippled within the first couple of days – Do you have some thin soled house shoes?

Yes, some moccasins.

You can start walking in those on a gravel road until it doesn't hurt then socks, then bare feet but it will take 2-3 months to get to where you need to be.

Very good advice – thanks.

Mike wants to know, "What is your destination?"

I haven't chosen one but it probably should have a good flint resource.

Harry chimes in, "Gault would be good, but so would the Alibates Flint Quarry."

Mike suggests, "I would go with Alabates – you would be on the High Plains and have some easily recognizable land marks with water and food resources."

Harry adds, "At least we think so – dependent on at what exact time you want to go back to."

I need your thoughts on that – we have some ranges but the pluses and minuses could put me in no man's land – literally.

Mike – Actually, we've narrowed the known Clovis sites down to a 500 year period somewhere between 12,800 and 13,300 calendar years before present so they were tromping around the area during that time – but it would probably be better to be there earlier than later but there are still a lot of questions about how numerous they were though.

Harry – OK, so we get you back there then what?

Bill – Wait a minute – why not drop him at Alabates?

Mike – I agree with that but as close to the kill date of the mammoths at Blackwater Draw as you can get. We know they were there for a long period and he can easily get there and back in a year.

Bill pulls a photo scale out of his Day Timer and measures the distance on the General's map. It's a little over 150 miles as the proverbial flies – 300 and change round trip.

Harry – How far to Gault?

Bill – Measures again.

Mike – I can tell you it's 500 plus.

Bill – 550, which is out of the question.

Rob – If they are at Blackwater Draw they will have been to Gault.

Harry – That's true – and may be going or have gone to Alabates.

Mike – True.

Harry – Back to reality – which none of this is – you are dumped on a pile of Alabates flakes and as you pull them out of your butt what's your next move?

Well IF there is someone there I would prefer to pick my own time to reveal myself so I hope it will be night – I guess I can pick the time of day – they didn't say – I would look for campfires and dependant on the weather try to find some shelter.

Bill – Wait, wait, wait – you've got to mark THAT SPOT!

You're right – I really need to mark it before I go – at least in my mind – and get a current GPS reading for them to have here.

Mike – You probably need to helicopter over the whole route.

That's a good idea.

Harry – Then?

I'll have to find materials for an atlatl and darts and knap some points and tools.

Mike – When was the last time you made a Clovis Point?

Probably, now – 20 years ago.

Mike – I remember you did pretty well but you better start practicing.

You're right – I bet with these connections I can get some raw material.

Harry – I don't know – NPS is still THE Independent Agency in Government.

Mike – They confiscate stuff all the time from hikers so I'm sure they have some misplaced flakes big enough to work.

Harry – OK, you've found shelter made a weapon and are starving to death

Yeah, probably – so I start hunting.

Bill – How long has it been since you've eaten some tainted meat?

Geeze Bill, I'm not sure, I don't go out looking for it – pause – but that's a good point I may have to scavenge on some leftovers from something else's meal.

Bill – I would try to get some of those bacteria in my gut before I left.

Rob looks at the floor and doesn't say anything.

Harry – I guess you know this is completely crazy – the whole damn idea – Something is going to kill and/or eat your pink ass as soon as you get there.

Bill - That does bring up the most imposing question of all – the actual contact with these people. First and primary you cannot, under any circumstances, alter the future in any way.

What do you mean?

Bill – You can't kill one of them, produce any offspring, show them any improvements in their hygiene or tools or anything else that would change the existing circumstances of any individual or group of individuals.

Long silence.

Mike – Bill is right you will be going as an observer only not as a participant, even in their survival – you can't even save one of them even if you could.

Harry – His advantage and maybe his only one, is that he is going to look a LOT older than any of their elders which will evoke some awe if not respect.

Bill – That's true, if someone has survived to his age they may revere him and to some degree take care of him. That's common in primitive societies that modern man has observed and recorded.

Knock on the door – Rob opens –

It's Ferguson, "Lunch is ready for you in the conference room."

Mike – I knew I was getting hungry but hadn't even looked at the time.

The restrooms are down the hallway past the conference room.

Harry and Mike are conversing at the urinals.

Mike – What do you think his chances are?

Harry – Less than 50%.

Mike – Do you think we should bring that up?

Harry – Would you want to know that?

Mike – Nope.

They all sit down to salad, fresh baked yeast rolls, T-bones, baked potatoes, pinto beans and cobbler for dessert.

Mike – Darn good of you to put on this feed for us old friend.

Rob – Anytime.

Small talk about each other's lives and current projects – Rob learns they have been given $25,000 each to come for the meeting but must follow up with reports separately and evaluate Rob's experiences when, and if, he makes it back.

Back at the General's office all breakfast leavings have been cleaned up and a portable white board with dry markers is in place.

Rob – Let's get back to my actual contact.

Bill – Wait a minute – how are you going to mark the days so you will know exactly what day to be back?

Well, I thought I would find a good solid staff and place daily cut marks on it.

Bill – That's good, but remember, even if sick or injured THAT is your first priority.

Understood.

Harry – What if one of the fathers offers a daughter as a mate – what do you do?

I...

Mike – I've got an idea – point to your privates and hold out your index finger and let it droop that's universal regardless of the time period.

Bill – That's good, but what about the language barrier?

That concerns me greatly – how do I communicate?

Harry – Do you talk in your sleep?

Not that I know about but Della wears ear plugs because of my snoring.

Bill – Then not likely – George is probably the best I know of on primitive languages but that doesn't mean we can even come close to what theirs was.

Mike – They may think at his age he may have a hearing problem – and that can be used to an advantage.

21

Bill – That's good – and simple observation and nodding of head will suffice at first – but don't appear to them that you are on your death quest – they may accommodate you.

Harry – I sure would like to know their burial practices – especially when they were out on the Plains.

Mike – We all want to know everything you can bring back – by the way let your beard grow out. You don't want to look like you've been trimming it.

The General knocks on the door and enters, "I hope this has been productive but it is almost 3 and we have 2 planes waiting to take you back to your respective home bases and want to respect the amount of time you have already provided to help us with this program."

Each thank the General and he asks Rob to stay a minute longer – each of the colleagues give their best wishes to Rob.

Was your time with your colleagues helpful?

Absolutely – they helped immensely and we agreed to keep the conversation going via email.

Good – and what is your thinking at this point, most importantly have you had any indication as to your wife's feelings on the matter?

Yes I have – she said she would stand behind my decision especially if she gets to stay at the Broadmoor – laughter.

That's good and where are you with your decision?

Rob pauses for a moment – I'm honored by the offer and confidence in me to make this awesome journey fraught with all the dangers equivalent to what any human has ever encountered and all the possible complications of getting back but – I accept the challenges and will begin preparing for it immediately.

I am pleased. I know we have chosen the right man – I likewise will have our people follow up on all the necessary details to provide for your departure. The Colonel will take you to the plane and will be your first responder but I am at the other end of the line if you have any questions he can't answer or any problems that seem to be going awry – Hands him his card.

Thank you General – I will do my best to fulfill the mission.

I know you will.

The trip back was quick. Rob was very introspective saying very little. He bid farewell and thanks to Ferguson and went directly home. Seeing it perhaps for the first time from a totally new perspective – he stops a moment before driving up the lane – Della was waiting for him at the door.

Well?

Well – I told them I would do it.

I thought you would. You have never backed down from a challenge in your life – I spent a sleepless night but still stand behind you.

He gives her a long hug and kisses her deeply.

Come on in, I've got supper ready. He couldn't stop talking about the experience and she listened dutifully. They skype Nita who is overseas doing post-doctoral work and after a lengthy explanation by her dad she concurs with his decision with surprising acceptance but with the admonition that she is kept up on all the details by email acknowledging she will be getting all the negatives from her mother and all the positives from her father.

The next day he spent time writing his report to the General and started walking in his house shoes. He called the Alabates Flint Quarries National Monument and talked to the Director. Rob said he needed some large flakes for educational purposes and was told he could come pick out what he needed so he called the local school district which readily agreed to multiple demonstrations. In his report back to the General he mentioned the desire to helicopter the route his colleagues had proposed.

Within the week the Colonel called to set the date – they arranged for a time and Rob met the pilot at the Peterson Air Force Base. They flew to Amarillo and refueled. They quickly got to the Alabates National Monument and had arranged to land in the parking lot before the park opened. The Director met them and Rob picked out a box of fine large flakes to take with them. While they were there he took several GPS readings on locations he thought would work and took pictures and knew he could find them on Google. There were still no visitors by the time they left and their heading was set for Clovis, New Mexico. They made a wide circle around the Quarry with Rob taking digitals flying over Lake Meredith which was formed from the Canadian River where much earlier Castaneda, Coronado's chronicler during the Spanish entrada in 1541 described plentiful fruits, nuts & berries.

They crossed a wide expanse of low hills and gullies and then onto the Llano Estacado with hundreds of playas, now dry lakebeds, until they got to upper Palo Duro Canyon with a few seep springs still visible. They continued southwest to Terria Blanca Creek that runs into Frio Draw then over the headwaters of Running Water Draw to a little southwest of Clovis where they turned east back down Blackwater Draw to the site where he had worked as a

Grad student. They flew right over the Blackwater Draw National Historic Landmark then turned north to the Cannon Air Force Base to fuel up.

This was a great opportunity as he had never seen this country from the air much less a copter and he took hundreds of digitals. He didn't know if they could make it back to the Colorado Springs on a tank of gas but the pilot said, "No problem". He asked if they could fly over the Folsom Type Site, excavated in the 1920's becoming the first proven evidence that humans were associated with Pleistocene megafauna in North America and was assured they could – a tremendous experience. Over the next few weeks Rob tries to get ready for the departure including emails and phone calls with his colleagues as well as a presentation and flint knapping demonstration to the Intro Anthropology class at the Air Force Academy.

Della picks out her room at the Broadmoor and he goes back to NASA to meet with a memory expert and Dr. Ellis to discuss the exact relocation site. He gets a major physical and meets with the General and the Colonel again and gets his three teeth pulled by a beautiful young dentist. He calls his colleagues and visits a long time with his good, career long friend, Mike.

Don't be in any rush to leave Alabates if there is good water and game. You'll need to have time to make some clothing and prepare for the trip. You know this whole thing is crazy, if not insane and I think you are a damned fool for going through with it.

Yes, Della says the same thing.

She's right you know – but I've got to tell you if I had the chance, I'd go too – just get back safe Buddy.

I'm going to do my best to do just that.

Rob and Della arrive at NASA on May 5th for Rob to go through all the pre-teleportation countdown procedures and to show Della the process where she says, "I'm not going to watch your remains be vacuumed up, besides I've seen you naked."

Rob goes to a tanning salon for the first time in his life at the recommendation of Dr. Baker so he won't look so white and/or be so vulnerable to the sunlight.

That night their sex is good and Della tells him again he had better not be fooling around with any of those Prehistoric women and he responds with, "But honey, they ARE Prehistoric, besides I'm just an observer."

You can look but don't touch.

Yes 'mam, I promise.

As the day arrives he tries to sleep in but rest is elusive and he goes over his last minute desires with Della in case he doesn't get back but she gets very despondent so he cuts it short. They relive the good times reminiscing about special trips and family pets and discuss keeping the Hogan as their sanctuary no matter how much money they have especially for Nita and her children if she ever gets around to that.

Even though the send off was scheduled for 9PM they wanted him to be there at 6PM so he says goodbye to Della who states for the hundredth time, "Be careful!"

He gets there a little ahead of time. They had everything calibrated to 13,000 calendar years before the present which was toward the end of the concentration of Carbon 14 dates for the Clovis Period occupation at Blackwater Draw. Dr. Baker gives him a last quick check over and Dr. Ellis pulls him aside and says, "just in case you miss the first year and heaven forbid you miss the second year, don't give up, come back the third year and give us a couple of days on each side of the date and stay there. We will have improved our technology and even with the changes in the in the solar system we will probably be able to correlate the variations enough to bring you back.

That's good to know Dr. – pretty sure I'll keep that in mind – THANKS!
Good luck!
Thanks again for everything.
They shake hands.

# Chapter 3

# The New World

There was somebody at each station and two guys in total coverage white suits wipe him down EVERYWHERE – and he enters the chamber – Of course not knowing how many of the personnel were making comments about his manhood but those antibacterial towels were cold after all.

The actual experience was momentary like being under anesthesia. He was little dazed when he first landed but he was still upright – It was dark but a quarter moon and the stars gave some ambient light – He did not see any campfires so he piled three rocks on top of each other until he could find a more permanent marker – but he could tell it was one of the three mounds they decided would be best because it was more isolated. He did not see any of the numerous quarries that were there when he visited the site – 13,000 years later! It just hit him he was back – for better or worse. He made his way up the canyon to a small overhang he had chosen during the flyover in which to spend the first night, his feet did well after their toughening. The place was smaller due to the lack of erosion – but still adequate protection enough to spend the rest of the night.

He noticed the temperature –it was mild and a little more humid than his time period. The shelter had a sandy floor so he roughed out a sleeping place and tried to get some rest because he knew he would need it – he could see the stars looking just under the roofline – they were spectacular like being on top of the mountains – he suddenly felt very alone, but settled in for a fitful sleep. He heard some, various noises but they were far away and indistinguishable.

He awoke with first light – he realized he had been rejuvenated. He really could breathe better, hear better, smell better and even see better or maybe that was just the lack of pollution.

He makes his way down the slope and hears the distinct sounds of knapping flint – he cautiously makes his way around the edge of the draw – the wind was in his face and he could smell him first – not like a homeless person – more like a fresh untanned animal hide – he sees him – a Clovis person! His back was to him – so he was totally unaware of Rob's presence – the first thing he noticed was the reflection of sunlight off the man's partially balding head.

He was using the angle of the sunlight to knap large blades – Clovis blades – a pile of them were stacked next to him – he had on a vest of tanned hide and a skirt – couldn't tell if it had legs or not and he couldn't see his face – He didn't want the 6th sense to kick in so he stopped looking and made his way back around the edge of the draw.

He sat down in front of "his" shelter and took some deep breaths. Balding! – Very rare in early Asians but not uncommon in early Europeans – Should he make him aware of his presence? He's naked for God's sake! It suddenly hit him – this man is the resident knapper – he stays here and produces blades in exchange for what? Food, letting him live – was he here because of his age or an injury, or was this his duty? Too many unknowns at this point – probably judicious to go back up the Canadian and get a little better prepared to meet these people socially. He made his way up the bank, far enough away so as not to alert the knapper. He had easily found a flake sharp enough to cut a green limb and sharpens it so it could easily be driven into the ground. He goes back to his landing spot and drives the stake where the three rocks were piled. He still couldn't see any other humans or habitation areas – he makes his way on up the Canadian – from his vantage point he could view a vast expanse but still couldn't see any game.

As he traveled further up river he could see there had been a flood recently – large limbs were lodged against one another at the bends and numbers of small mammals were lodged in the debris but far too decomposed to utilize, even their skins – he saw catfish and perch in the pools but still needed some implements to survive. Everything so far had been willows and cottonwoods and small junipers. Finally there was a whole old oak – plenty of material to choose from. The only thing he had with him is the large flake – so he begins to make an atlatl and finds a straight limb long enough to make a spear which would also become his calendar staff and shapes it to a sharp point. His energy level is amazing, like they said he feels 20 years younger. He picks out half a dozen good willow limbs for darts hoping he can find some good cane later. He stashes his artifacts and goes back to the three hills where he selects some good flakes and a quartzite cobble to use as a hammer stone hoping for an antler later to use as a billet and flaking tool. He went back up the bank so his knapping wouldn't be heard by the other knapper.

He is able to make a couple of decent points and a knife, scraper, awl combination. He attaches the points to the darts using willow bark but still doesn't have sinew or any feathers for fletching and no pouch to carry his "possibles". But he was getting hungry – nothing to eat going on 2 days – he starts heading up-river looking for anything that might be salvageable from the flood – around one of the bends he sees an incredible sight. 4 bison piled up in what would have been an eddy – a calf, a juvenile and 2 adults – the stench was overpowering – But he had to see if there was anything he could use – hide, sinew, horn, bone or meat – all of a sudden the juvenile moved and gasps, maybe his last, he stuck the staff into the chest. It didn't even struggle but it had been alive and that was important. He dragged it out of the pile but couldn't get it any further. He started to skin and quarter the animal keeping the back skin in one piece – It took until dark to get everything out of the bottom to a tree where he could put the quarters in forks but knew they could attract predators so he took the heart and liver to another rock shelter he had seen.

He got some juniper bark and wood and started a fire with sparks from the quartzite hammer stone and flint. He roasted some of the heart and liver – it was tough and strong but without a doubt nutritious and gave him some energy. He thought about the first day – all the circumstances that have made his immediate future much better. He slept better until he heard growling toward the stash of meat – hopefully they didn't get it all. The next morning he snuck up downwind to the tree. No animals but the two quarters that were in the lower forks of the tree were gone. The hide and other forequarter and hind quarter were OK but he had to find a better and safer location soon. He found another large cottonwood tree further upstream and began cutting thin strips from what was left and hanging them as high as possible to dry. After a full day he had only the bones remaining except for the head and a radius and ulna which he took to fashion fore shafts. He staked out the hide with the flesh side up and roasted some loin and ate some berries he had found that evening but they were a little green which he was soon to regret. The new shelter he had found was comfortable and defendable, smoke drafted up and out – smoke! That could draw visitors either wanted or unwanted. He decided to go back downstream toward the quarry the next morning to check further out his neighbor.

He passed the bison assemblage and where he had placed the quarters most of the bones and entrails were gone. He took his time slowly making his way along the north bank as he came to a bend the footing was precarious and he was looking down at the trail – when he looked up there was the balding Paleo Man looking at him about 25 yards away. He had a reddish brown beard but not bushy like his after it had grown out. He was probably 5'8" tall and stocky built. His vest was tied in front with rawhide and his tanned hide dress was like a kilt almost down to his knees and his moccasins were squared toed, sewn in front. He was carrying an atlatl and a couple of darts and had a possibles bag over his shoulder. He was not young, probably in his mid-30's. He had a bad scar on the left side of his face, but he certainly was not Asian. Rob knew he must look just as strange – naked for starters but with a bushy white beard and slightly tanned skin – but different for sure. They stared at each other for what seemed like several minutes but it was probably only a minute. Rob put up his hand as to say hello, but with that the man turned and headed back toward where he had seen him originally. No sense in following as that could produce a defensive posture or action. Besides he now knows that the Paleo Man had seen the smoke and now knows who he is. So he turned and went back up to his shelter.

He started scraping the meat from the hide. It went well, maybe a little too well. He picked up a corner and the hair was starting to slip. It would not make a robe for winter but if he hurried it could make some clothing, a possibles bag, rawhide string and maybe some moccasins.

He had already put aside as much sinew as he could strip from the forequarter and the hindquarter. He secured the points he had made to the willow darts but he was pretty sure he would be able to replace them hafting the points to reed darts soon.

He was beginning to fix two meals a day. Noon and evening and the coals from his fire kept the shelter pleasant at night. He worked hard the rest of the day and got the meat side scraped down. He would turn it tomorrow and do the furred side which would be much more difficult.

He would take breaks and go up to the ridge above the shelter and see if he could see anyone or any game. On a couple of occasions he could see small herds of animals but they were too far away to determine species.

He spotted a grove of what looked like fruit trees of some kind in a tributary running into the Canadian from the southwest. He could see his jerky tree and everything seemed OK. He had seen swallows, sparrows, larks, doves and a few other hawk size birds at a distance but nothing really large yet. He had also noticed lots of small mammal tracks in the river bottom but he certainly could be announcing his presence with all of his activities thus far.

He worked the next couple of days on the hide and the hair came off easier than expected but he was concerned that he didn't have salt or tannin but he did have brains! Bison brains, that he will have to retrieve tomorrow. Sleep comes easily – he feels the Paleo Man would wait for reinforcements before he comes back.

He went back to the bison pile early the next morning. The skull of the juvenile was still there even though there was little else except a couple of very large vultures that were scavenging on the remains and flew off with difficulty. Tracks indicated it was at least one BIG wolf – Dire! The hair stood up on the back of his neck and he started to be very wary. He separated the head from the remaining skeletal parts and took it back to his camp. It was very heavy and not easy breaking into the brain cavity but once accomplished the decomposition had already begun which was a relief because usually it requires boiling to get it down to consistency that it can be spread over the cleaned hide. He was able to do one side that day and would wait until it dries before doing the other side.

It was starting to cloud up in the southwest and he realized that he had been most fortunate to have achieved so much thus far because he had experienced good weather. He decided to go ahead and gather the jerky before it got wet – he could always put it back up. He had made several trips before the storm hit with a force he had seldom seen in his lifetime. The river was almost immediately turned into a raging torrent carrying brush and trees downstream. He took refuge in his shelter which was facing south but the east side was hit hard. Fortunately his fire and hide were in the western half but he would have to find a dryer place to sleep and keep the fire going because it was already getting cold. The storm lasted well into the night and was fierce with light-ening, hail and very strong winds.

The next morning there was water standing on the east side of the shelter but everything else was dry. However, the hide wasn't even close to being dry so he decided to take it up to the ridge as soon as there was sunshine again. But this was some kind of low-pressure system. The rain lasted two more days but not as strong and only a mist the third day. Rob left the remaining jerky in the tree to see if it would dry out enough to use later. He took the hide up on the ridge and placed it on a large limestone out-cropping and weighted it down with rocks.

The next few days were perfect. Cloudless, mild and not too humid and the grass was greening up more each day. By going up on the ridge more often he began to see more animals and that made sense. They were following the late spring rains. He saw small bunches of bison, camels & horses but no large predators but they will be following the herds soon which meant he probably needed to start his journey to Blackwater Draw.

The timing seemed to be right. All he needed now was a tanned hide. He was able to turn the hide and get the remaining brains on the other side and it dried quickly. However, all of the remaining jerky was not salvageable. But what he saved only needed a little more time in the sun. He found a low hang-ing oak limb and stripped and smoothed it to be able to finish the hide by working it back & forth until it became pliable.

This all went as planned and he was able to cut out a vest, skirt and moc-casins with just enough left to make his possibles pouch. He also had plenty of rawhide to sew the pieces together and made an awl from part of the ulna. It took a full day but he was at last covered.

He went back to the quarry to get some more flakes but didn't see the Paleo Man. He decided something may have happened to him during the flooding. As he made his way around the edge of the draw where he had first seen him he could see the pile of blades had been scattered but no sign of any activity since the rains. He walked a little further down the ridge to look for his shelter. He could see a good overhang further downstream but no smoke coming from it and he couldn't tell if the water had gotten high enough to wash into it. He was concerned and his natural instincts were to search for him. But he remembered what his colleagues had said – that he could NOT alter the future by saving someone or killing someone.

So he left the blades which would have been nice to have and headed back to his camp. He was a little melancholy, it saddened him to think the Paleo Man might be dead or worse yet injured and needing help. But he had to turn his thoughts to Blackwater Draw, he really needed to observe the interactions of a Paleo group and everyone agreed that Blackwater Draw would probably be the best opportunity to do that. The trek to Alibates would probably be excursions by males to get resource material and not family units. He didn't feel it would be productive to stay at the quarry so he planned to depart the next morning. He decided ethically he could leave the bison skull with the chopped hole in the forehead buried in the shelter because that was a legitimate thing they would have done.

He ventured up the tributary where he had seen the fruit trees which turned out to be plums but still too green. He did however find some last year's pecans. He continued up river until it headed west then he turned southwest entering the Llano Estacado described by Coronado's chronicler Castaneda as a land of limitless grass and sky that merged in the distance with no landmarks causing disorientation to be common.

The first 40 miles would be one of the greatest challenges. While he had salvaged the bison bladder and it was full of water but it was fragile, he could only hope it would last until he could replace it. His first available water may not be until he gets to the upper Palo Duro Canyon. There have always been questions by him and his colleagues as to the possibility that the Playas had fresh seasonal rain water until salinity started to accumulate making it brackish and undrinkable at some point.

It would probably be tomorrow before he could find out as he was still in the Canadian River breaks at the end of the first day. There was another heavy storm to the north but looked to be far enough away that he would only get some downdraft wind from it.

It was already getting cooler so he found some wood and a place to set up camp at the upper end of a draw on a fairly high terrace. At some point he sure would like a warm robe especially to sleep in.

As he marked another day on his spear and realized it had been almost a month into his arrival back in time. It had gone better than expected – a lot better. As Harry had predicted, the weather, before the beginning of the Younger Dryas, was probably milder in both summers and winters but with more numerous and intense storms. He had made about 12 miles the first day even though it was not easy traversing the draws and gullies. By his calculations

33

he was northwest of where Amarillo would eventually be and he would be up on the High Plains tomorrow.

The storm passed but the wind was chilly. He was glad to have the fire. He thought he heard a mammoth trumpet but it was very far away. He did notice a lot more "shooting stars" than he normally did back home and wondered if it was the Merced or some unknown long past meteor shower from a terminal comet. He would have to ask a paleoastronomer – he laughed – when he started his career there were just archaeologists – period. But it's better now, more of these young professionals are finding jobs in a lot more specific areas of research and that was good for the profession as a whole. He was tired and rested well.

He awoke because of a sixth sense sensation, kind of like right before you see the rattlesnake that hasn't rattled yet. He moved slowly, carefully and looked up the draw and below him but as he slowly raised himself up above the edge of the precipice and saw, walking directly away from him was a giant cat. He couldn't tell if it was the American lion or a sabertooth because he couldn't see a profile but his suspicion was it was a carmel-colored lion. They were definitely larger than the sabertooth "tigers" even though the sabertooths were probably not tiger in pattern or color. The cat never turned to look back – maybe most fortunately. He didn't know why the cat hadn't consumed him during the early morning hours because it certainly could have. Maybe he had encountered humans previously and was just curious or wasn't hungry. Either way he felt most fortunate. He gathered his things and set out toward the upper end of Palo Duro Canyon. The breaks flattened out to what was easily recognizable as the Llano Estacado – flat and treeless with no vertical infringements – calf-high grass that looked to be a supersized side oats gramma what every modern day rancher's dreams are made of. He could easily see why mammoths, bison, camels and horses would be attracted to this area, as well as all the predators that would be following in their paths.

He could see a fairly large depression to the west so he diverted to see if it was a Playa lake and what a lake it was! With numerous shorebirds, ducks and other species, he saw some whitetail deer run south when he approached and large sandhill cranes flew north into the wind. As he got closer rabbits, ground squirrels, prairie dogs and burrowing owls were abundant and at the water's edge frogs, horseshoe crabs and fairy shrimp. This had to be fresh water – he bent down and scooped up a handful it was slightly brackish but certainly drinkable like the water from the shallow windmills along the front range of

34

the Rockies. He filled his bison bladder adding to what remained of the good Canadian water.

As he sat at the edge of the Playa lake he saw many of the same species he would if he were back in his time – redwing blackbirds, curlews, swallows, sparrows, meadowlarks, lark buntings, horned larks – as he looked down a bull snake was making its way along the shoreline, he decided that would make a good meal so he speared it and quickly skinned it. He built a fire and roasted it. It was a sweet white meat – quite good.

He decided to camp there – maybe for a couple of days and try to mentally record all comings and goings especially during the early morning and late evening hours. He didn't have to wait long – a small herd of 4 horned antelope appeared on the opposite side of the lake, nervously drank and left. They were almost identical to the Pronghorn he had hunted and taken out on the eastern plains of Colorado – but they were larger and the prong was actually another part of the horn jutting upward and outward at the top.

Just about dark a group of horses came in from the south. They were not as large as most of our modern riding and working horses – they were stocky and pretty heavily furred – like the remaining Siberian Steppe specimens he had seen on the Nova and Discovery channels.

It suddenly got very quiet and he got very still too. At the north side where a small draw ran into the lake he saw a familiar shape – it was probably the big lion he had seen that morning. He came down, drank, looked around and left. It definitely was not a sabertooth, but perhaps even scarier considering its size.

He decided to build the fire bigger and sleep close with extra wood at hand. There were willows and cottonwoods primarily on the southeast edge. It dawned on him that it may be a seep spring although the fresh water on top may be from the recent rains. Once again he thought he heard a mammoth trumpet, twice or maybe two different ones, but it was far away and he couldn't be sure.

It was a restless night but he slept past sunrise and was awakened by the noises of the morning which included a lot of splashing. He peered out from the cane and saw a large herd of elk and the yearlings were out in the water jumping, splashing and playing with each other. It looked like a great opportunity to add some fresh meat to the possibles pouch. He carefully made his way around the edge of the Playa staying below the tops of the cattails and reeds and actually got close enough to try to kill one of the smaller animals. He had to stand up to launch the dart with the atlatl and when he did the whole herd stopped and stared at him just long enough to get off the shot. It hit one of the young elk in the foreleg but knocked it down. He ran up and slit the juggler with the knife edge of his multiple purpose flint tool. The rest of the herd ran up to the edge of the depression that made the Playa, turned and watched him get the young one out of the water then trotted out of sight. He quickly gutted and skinned the animal. He was able to work well into dark with the full moon and was finally able to roast some of the fresh liver and heart. It seemed particularly good late that night and he slept well even though he was concerned that the lion was still within smelling range of the kill.

He left the skeleton, legs and other internal organs where he had taken what he needed. He cut the rest into large strips, packed them into the fresh rolled up hide and slung it over his shoulder with some of his rawhide. He left early the next morning just as light was breaking under the clouds. He looked back at the Playa as it was coming alive with activity. It was humid and smelled fresh. It was unique, with new odors both pungent and sweet. He knew he needed more vegetable matter so he began to follow his nose looking for green sustenance. The pungency was easy to find – the same buffalo gourds that grow throughout the southwestern portion of the U.S. Another, almost non-odoriferous squash looking vine was loaded with small fruit but they were still green and hard. It would be late summer before they could be eaten, but it was becoming obvious that there were, at this particular time period, plenty of resources for these people. IF the winters were not too severe their population should be increasing. He walked rapidly across the prairie but as the clouds burned off the sun was intense and he felt his skin get hot. If the circumstances had been more predictable at the Playa he would have stayed longer and tanned the elk hide. It was small and lighter than the Bison and he wanted to keep the hair on it so he made an immediate decision to go ahead and flesh it out. He staked it out with yucca stalks and the cleaning went quickly. He was very hot by the time he finished so he got some larger yucca stalks and put the hide flesh side up to catch the drying of the sun. He crawled underneath the shade it made. He napped in spurts aware that the smell could attract a variety of curious predators who might want more than a fresh hide.

He got up as the sun was setting. The moon was already bright so he decided to keep working his way toward the canyon. It was still easy walking and he made good time.

He kept looking for something that would offer a secure location. Then he saw it – a camp fire! He was about a hundred yards away and he couldn't see anyone moving around but it was late probably around midnight. He certainly wasn't going to walk in on them. That would have been offensive at least, dangerous at worst. He was excited but concerned – How would he introduce himself? How would he approach them? How does he communicate with them? How is he going to spend the rest of the night? He decided to back a little further away and observe their morning activities before making a move.

His sleep was fitful and he was dozing when he thought he heard human voices. He stood up and picked up his gear and started walking toward their camp. As he got closer he could see they were already packed up and on the move. A young boy saw him and called to the rest of the group. They all turned and looked at him. He stopped and held up his hand as if to say hello. They looked at each other then at him for what seemed like minutes but it all occurred quickly. The three adult males, six females and three small children and two juveniles including the boy who had seen him first turned and walked swiftly toward the southwest. The boy waved at him before turning to go with the rest. He waved back.

He watched them until they disappeared over the horizon and made his way down where they had camped. Obviously they carried wood with them and there were still live coals in their fire. He stoked it and got enough fire to roast some of the fresh elk. He could tell there were six distinct sleeping areas but little other evidence that they had ever been there. He thought about staying at the location for a while but it really didn't offer the needed shade or security so he continued due south with Blackwater Draw as his goal.

# Chapter 4

## Contact

He found a tributary running south. He was pretty sure it was one of many that would end up in the headwaters of Palo Duro Canyon. It got deeper with high limestone walls but there were no shelters at this point. As he got further down the arroyo he could hear running water but it was still below him and he came to a high drop off with a creek at the bottom. There were lots of large trees, cottonwoods, willows, pecan and numerous bushes and vines. As he was surveying the scene before him he heard growling and fighting with more than one animal involved and since he couldn't get down at this location he decided to climb out and stay on the rim of the canyon to investigate the argument. He made his way along the edge looking and listening. He could hear crunching of bone then he saw them – half a dozen Dire wolves scavenging on a very large old Bison bull – They were huge – far bigger than he could have ever imagined – long legged with paws that looked as big as man-hole covers – a third bigger than the largest modern wolf he had ever seen. They were feeding on their kill and were not looking up. He slowly sat down but was uneasy even with the wind in his favor. Although the wolves were occupied and he didn't see how they could get up the higher walls of the canyon, he didn't want to take any chances.

He was pretty sure they would stay with the kill especially since it was near water. He continued on up the creek and found a shelter but it was on the other side of the canyon. He surveyed the possible route down and back up to the shelter, although difficult it was doable.

The creek was not a problem and with a great deal of effort he made it to the shelter. It had been used previously. Several fire pits and bedding areas but not recently. He found a few flakes and a broken billet made from an elk antler, but again they weren't leaving much in the way of retrievable material culture, now or in the future. He staked out the elk hide so it would catch some sunlight and gathered a stash of wood. He cut the remaining elk meat into strips for jerky except for what he roasted that night. It was comfortable and secure and he slept well. He decided to stay there for a few days. The elk hide dried quickly and he was able to rub in its brains he had brought with him in the old bison bladder.

He was able to find some ripe early grapes and last year's pecans and locate a flock of turkeys that were roosting in an old dead cottonwood. He lay in wait as they flew in that evening getting close enough to spear one of the jakes among the low perching birds. He stowed some of the feathers for fletching and put the turkey on a green willow spit and roasted it whole. It was especially good and it lasted a couple of days.

He also found some perch in one of the larger pools and was able to spear a few of the larger ones. He packed them in clay and baked them. They were also a pleasant change. It was hard to believe the journey was going so well – but there was still the apprehension of the unknown every day and night and he thought about and missed Della especially in those dark hours.

The shelter was shady & cool during the heat of the day. The smoke drafted up and out at all times- It would also make a good place to stay during the winter. He would remember how to get back to it.

One night he heard the growling again and then howling that was so loud it hurt his ears. The Dire wolves were right below the shelter and they had probably smelled his scent but they kept moving on up the creek.

It was definitely time to continue his trek toward Blackwater Draw. He took another day to gather nuts and berries this time downstream. He found a wide heavily used trail crossing the canyon. Bison tracks dominated the numerous species and he would add his to the mix the next morning.

He had finished tanning the elk hide so he could bundle most of his goods in it and sling it over his shoulder so he was ready to set out on the next leg of his journey in this time warp.

As he got close to the trail crossing the canyon he heard voices. There was a group led by a large male about 5'10", stocky and muscular, but not fat by any means. He was almost bald with graying tuffs of reddish brown hair on the temples and back of the head. He was dressed much like the Paleo Man he had seen at the quarry, tailored shirt and skirt. He also wore the same square toed moccasins. He had a highly polished atlatl smoothed from heavy use and what looked to be half a dozen reed darts with feather fletching but only a few with fore shafts and points attached.

There were a couple of older women behind him making their way down the bank with several younger men and women behind them. The man stopped and held up his hand for the rest of the band to stop. They looked each other over a few minutes. The rest were transfixed over his strangeness – not in his clothing because it was similar but in the whiteness of his hair and beard.

The Big Guy had short reddish facial hair but not nearly as long as his, very much like the Paleo Man at the Alibates quarry.

Two of the younger men started toward him and the older man stopped them with a word – unrecognizable from anything he had encountered as a primitive language. The women were talking among themselves and pointing at him. He stood his ground unsure of what would happen next.

The Big Guy approached him and made a half salute motion – he did the same. The Big Guy said several words to him but none familiar. He had to act quickly but confidently. He pointed to his ears and shook his head negatively – as if to say he couldn't hear. The Big Guy said something back to the group – they obviously were discussing his future, if not fate.

The Big Guy turned and went back over to the group and listened to the others. He occasionally commented on their deductions. It looked like a split decision but The Big Guy started up the other bank and motioned for him to follow. The two men who were anxious about his presence at the beginning fell in right behind them. The rest followed in single line as he glanced back going up the bank he could see it was a larger "tribe" than the one he had seen earlier but Rob would have to wait for the chance to experience personal interaction to determine who was who in the cultural system.

Once they reached flat land he had to pick up his usual pace. These people really could move! He hoped he would be able to save face. They were headed southwest toward Blackwater Draw so IF he was accepted within the unit this would be an exceptional opportunity to observe representatives of the Paleo-indians – the Clovis people! This is why he took all the chances to return to this time period!

41

Sometime around dusk The Big Guy stopped and everyone had a job to do – a fire was built in minutes, the women had meat and a squash like fruit on stakes hanging just close enough to the flames to roast the meal.

Rob offered the last of his elk meat to The Big Guy who accepted it and gave it to one of the older women who added it to the rest of the food being cooked. The group conversed in low tones with occasional glances toward him, this was probably the first time in any of their lives they had ever encountered an outsider like him – IF they only knew!

Rob put his belongings a little further away from where the camp was being established but it looked like he had been accepted for the time being anyway.

There were seven males ranging in age from about 6 to 30 to The Big Guy who may be crowding 40. One of the two who had threatened him at first looked just like Patrick Stewart who played Star Treks' Captain Picard on the Spaceship Enterprise. So these individuals were not Mongoloid but very much Caucasoid in appearance, just as he and some of his colleagues had predicted. They were darker than he was but partly because they had been exposed to the elements their whole lives. He had not yet seen the three babies in the group that had been carried in pack sacks with slings on their mothers' sides. There were six adult women and four teenage girls. That would make their number about what would be expected for a nomadic population – enough for protection but not too many to outstrip the immediate resources as they traversed throughout their territory.

As they ate there was a glorious sunset that appeared to be dust or ash maybe from one of the volcanoes in Mexico to the south. The night was short as the group was up with the first light. They ate jerky and what appeared to be a trail mix of nuts, berries and seeds, maybe sunflower. They were on the march by sunup and Rob's older body was having trouble getting underway – Oh, for a pot of coffee! However, his obvious disabilities may play to his benefit if they culturally respect his advanced age and want him to stay with the group as a positive omen. But some may have suspected he was at an age to remove himself from another tribe and die on behalf of the whole. If that was the prevailing thought then he should be an outcast – a coward that had gone against tradition. Maybe The Big Guy was asking for some time to see if he could find out where Rob had come from and how he had lived so long. Either way he wanted to stay with the group as long as he could.

Here he was, finally actually living with Paleo people, they were a very cohesive unit, efficient and cooperative – roles were clearly understood and accepted. Based on sex and age the younger girls collected firewood, prepared the fire pits and helped the older women with the cooking and camp chores. The young boys pursued hunting small game and various gathering activities. As they prepared the meal the older women took charge and distributed the food proportionally according to size of the recipient. The Big Guy definitely had a couple of "wives". The two younger adult males were probably his sons by one or both of the women who stay with him. This fits the proposal by John Martin, a paleoethnographer that groups of early aboriginal people exchanged, or traded, males as much as females to assure that gene flow would not be compromised.

As he had time to look at each individual he noticed they were healthy with enormous energy and discipline. He continued to sleep a little away from their encampment and his silence seemed to be accepted even though they didn't know if it was self-imposed or physical.

They were traveling much further toward the west than he would have and he soon saw the reason for the direction they were taking. They came upon a large playa which had several springs running into it and the water was very drinkable. There were numerous ducks and a small flock of geese circling after they were disturbed but soon landed on the opposite side. He realized this was the large lake bed he had seen from the helicopter that was located on the western edge of the Llano Estacado which is known locally as the "Caprock". Now it made sense – they would follow the edge of the escarpment down to the upper part of Blackwater Draw. The advantage would be dependable springs escaping the Ogallala formation which during this period would have had a high water table.

They camped on the northeast side which was downwind from the lake from the prevailing southwesterly winds. It was obvious that the group needed more provisions so the next morning Rob became a part of a communal hunt. A half dozen camels were watering on the southwest side and some four horned antelope ran away from the southeast corner but The Big Guy and the two other men appeared to be uninterested and set out very purposefully toward the edge of the Caprock. Their objective was clear when they got there as you could see 180 degrees for miles to the west, south and north. There were numerous small ponds at the base of the escarpment where small depressions filled with the water running from springs along the edge. They could see small numbers of peccary, whitetail deer, horses, camels and a pack of the large wolves in the distance.

The Big Guy gave some instructions to the other two and they split up with Rob following The Big Guy. The other two went south and The Big Guy and Rob went straight off the edge. It was not too difficult and they had some cover from the juniper and pinyon pine growing along the edge. They jumped half a dozen elk but they stayed in the trees and went north. As they got down near the water a pair of peccary ran out but apparently confused since the rest had scattered. The peccary stopped and looked at them about 25 yards away. The Big Guy was to Rob's left so he cast his dart at the one on the right. Both peccaries fell at the same time. The Big Guy looked at Rob and smiled – Rob wanted to give thumbs up but simply nodded. They were much larger than the javelinas of Mexico and the southwest U.S.

Each of them grabbed a hind leg and started hauling them back up the Caprock. As they topped out they could see the other two guys dragging a whitetail buck toward them. It was still in velvet but by the end of the summer it would have been one of the biggest Rob had ever seen.

Everyone came out to greet the hunters and the young men took the peccaries and the women took the deer and in a matter of minutes had everything gutted and skinned and the internal organs salvaged.

They stripped everything out of the intestines, put it in a large turtle shell with water and began to drop some of the hot limestone rock from around the fire pit into it. It didn't take long before it was boiling and one of the older women took out a pouch from her possibles bag and threw some kind of mix into the pot. There was only one buffalo horn ladle and The Big Guy got the first opportunity but filled it and brought it over to Rob even though he was standing back away from the group. It was quite an honor and everyone was watching – Rob nodded and sipped a little – it was hot but not bad and with her mix that definitely had some salt added it tasted similar to pea soup. The ladle was then passed around from one person to another until it was all eaten.

The other hunters retold the events of the day to all several times and Rob was beginning to feel very much a part of the group. The women had staked out the hides and began fleshing them out at sunrise. The young men caught a bag full of frogs and collected some cattail tubers which were cooked in turtle shells in the same manner as the day before. The meat had already been cut up and hung on racks made from willow branches so it looked like they would be camped there for a while.

Rob took the time to rest, observe and walk back to the edge of the Caprock. He was able to locate where Interstate 40 would eventually come up, where the small town of San Jon would be built along old Route 66 and he was standing about where Coronado first saw the Great Plains in 1541 which probably looked like what Rob was experiencing currently. He was able to better evaluate the environs and decided they were too far south to encounter muskoxen, caribou, and moose but maybe bears and there were not enough of the large succulous trees at this latitude for sloths. But where were the mammoths? The woolies would be much further north but there should be *Mammuthus columbi* like those that were killed at Blackwater Draw during this time period.

The group built small lean-tos with some of the willows and reeds growing along the bank of the lake and took siestas during mid-afternoon. Rob built his own and may have rested a little longer than the others but it was a welcome respite from being so active since his arrival. They were still leaving very little in the way of artifacts that were meaningful in and around the campsite. Rob decided to bury the broken billet he had found in the shelter. Maybe, just maybe, he will be able to find it again – far into the future.

One morning the group was packing up and preparing to leave by the time Rob woke up. He had just enough time to change out his darts to reeds and attach the turkey feather fletching and get his stuff together to join in the departure in his now accepted place behind The Big Guy.

They continued in a southwesterly direction on down the Caprock but staying on top easing out on the points occasionally just to survey the landscape and see what game was in the area. The escarpment veered to the west but they stayed on course toward Blackwater Draw to the south. They got to the upper portion of Frio Draw, which was the last of the draws that ran northeast and into the Red River eventually. It did have water running in it and it had a very wide flood plain with lots of cottonwoods, oaks, willows, cattails, reeds and some fruit and nut trees but no pecans this far west. There was lots of game but because they were still in good shape with the recent kills they only took advantage of the frogs, snakes and small turtles. There seemed to be more excitement among members of the unit as the goal, which Rob still was assuming to be Blackwater Draw, was getting closer, however, they were in no rush and they set up lean-to shelters once again.

The Big Guy always seemed to be on the lookout for other groups, mammoths, or maybe that was just his role – to watch out for his people. They seemed not to be in a hurry to move on and they seemed to be waiting on something. As hard as he tried he still could not make any connections to their language. While they were not an unhappy bunch they were a serious people with very little laughter or celebration. On the other hand there were no hostilities or major disagreements. The children did what was asked or expected of them. The older women wore necklaces composed of bone, snail shells, ivory and select stones which looked like hematite, probably being added as the opportunity presented itself. One of the teenage girls had started her ornamentation with half a dozen pieces. The men and boys seemed content in expressing themselves through their weapons and tools. Rob's were comparable and they were still treating him as an equal but he remained somewhat apart with his own campsite and shelter.

Late one afternoon there was much commotion as the family unit made their way up the edge of the draw to greet another group approaching from the northeast. They didn't shake hands or even wave – they just acknowledged one another. There were about the same number as The Big Guy's band. They were also Caucasoid in appearance with reddish brown hair and bearded men and their dark skin also appeared to be mostly from exposure to the elements.

The new arrivals began to set up their camp in close proximity to where the group he was with had camped. Their leader was not as tall as The Big Guy but was also well built and husky. He came over with The Big Guy, looked Rob over. Rob assumed the presence of total confidence that comes with maturity and the New Guy finally nodded approval. The two talked a while and The New Guy returned to his encampment. The interaction between the groups proved to be most interesting – the teenagers got together but only by the different sexes, however, all the smaller children played together. The adult men sat in a circle and probably caught up on the events that transpired since they last met. The women worked preparing a big evening meal for everyone. Not uncommonly there was no mid-day meal. Individuals ate jerky and nuts or berries but no one went hungry. There seemed to be a relaxed atmosphere with no indication of outside threats or intrusions. They settled into a routine but Rob figured there needed to be a hunting party go out soon as the supplies must be getting sparse with this many to feed.

Sure enough the next morning the adult males were preparing to go out on a hunting expedition. The Big Guy motioned for Rob to join him. Rob had not shot his new reed darts but felt confident they would work well.

They went upstream and quickly ran out of the trees that were so prevalent where they were camping. They were traveling due west with the sunrise at their backs. The draw became much narrower and only a small amount of water was flowing in the channel. There were four men including Rob from The Big Guy's clan and four from The New Guy's group. As they got closer to the edge of the Caprock they split up with The Big Guy's party staying straight ahead and The New Guy's party taking a southwesterly course. Rob didn't see or hear any indication of a voice or motion designating the separation so they must have decided this as part of the plan before they left camp. They certainly knew what they were doing because as they came up to and could look below the escarpment they could see a fairly large herd of bison congregated around one of the small lakebeds. Some were dusting themselves while others were in the water and a few lying down. Now the challenge would be to bring one of these giant beasts down. Which one or ones would they pick? What would be the strategy of the approach? Who would be doing what in the process? Rob decided just to stay close to The Big Guy and play it out and do his best to contribute to the effort. Just as with the last hunt there were lots of juniper and pinyon pine growing on the slope so they made their way down toward the herd. Rob couldn't see The New Guy's bunch but he was sure they were on the south side setting up to take an animal either by surprise or ambush one as it came by. It looked like The Big Guy, Rob and their two companions would take the lead since they were moving straight in. The wind was in their favor blowing from the southwest and they got within 30 yards of an old cow who was half asleep chewing her cud. A younger cow which was a little closer must have caught some motion and she stood up looking straight at them – she was quartering away from Rob but he took a chance and shot his dart right behind the shoulder if it didn't hit a rib it should be a lethal hit. The Big Guy also cast his dart and it hit square on the shoulder. The whole herd was off and running. The younger cow stumbled and almost went down but joined in the stampede but Rob could see she was bleeding from the wound he had made. His group followed the herd and met up with The New Guy's hunters. Apparently they had also got a dart in one of the slower moving bulls as they passed by their position evidenced by the tracks and blood. Everyone started in on tracking the injured game. The cow was down and dying. One of the younger men slit her throat with a hafted blade. Rob thought they would pursue the bull but they started skinning and quartering the cow. They separated the various parts that could be carried easily and left the quarters and hide and they all headed back to camp. They were joyously received. After the various partials were stored the entire assemblage headed for the kill site. They made short order of boning out the meat and dispensing it according to weight to each individual. Some of the bones, the hide and head were taken back for the marrow, brains, horns and fore shaft material. There was almost nothing remaining at the kill site. The intestines were stripped into several small containers and the bladder and almost all internal organs would be utilized. As with the previous kills there was the sharing of the soup and reenactment of the hunt. Rob got lots of credit but tried to play it down. Although The Big Guy's point broke on impact he kept his point and The Big Guy's broken tip he found during the butchering process. They all stayed up late around a common campfire. It was a memorable time. The next morning the hunters took to the field again to get on the trail of the bull. They encountered deer, elk, and peccaries but it was clear the objective was finding the bull. It wasn't hard to pick up the tracks but they never caught up to the herd or the bull. Rob wasn't sure how they would have handled another large animal that far away from the camp. Would they move to the new kill site or would they only take what they could carry easily? It was almost dark before they got back and the fresh meat had been roasted and was ready to eat. Rob felt good about his contribution but had he stepped over that fine line of not influencing the outcome or survival of an individual or in this case the entire group? He decided that as much game that they had encountered and as good as these guys were at hunting he hadn't changed a thing. They stayed at this location through August taking advantage of the shade, water, small game and ripening fruit, nuts and berries. The hunters made forays south to Running Water Draw which was a major tributary to the eastern edge of the Llano Estacado and eventually the Brazos river drainage. Rob was sure there would be a concentration of Paleo-people at the Lubbock Lake site just as there would be at Blackwater Draw and decided if The Big Guy's and The New Guy's groups decided not to travel in that direction he would stay on his objective to see Blackwater Draw during this time period. He was selective in what he gathered and put up a great deal of nuts, dried fruit and choice jerky utilizing some of their salt for taste and preservation. He still had not seen a source but they had given him a small bag full, which he used only a limited amount for his needs. The hot sun had allowed him to produce some raisins and prunes so he was ready to strike out for Blackwater Draw but would wait and see what The Big Guy was going to do. This had been a major encampment and there was a great deal more evidence of their occupation than at any of the other sites. There were fire hearths, broken bone, resharpening flakes and most probably a few lost or discarded artifacts. It would be hard to find this exact spot after almost 13,000 years but he did bury the tip of The Big Guy's point at his shelter. Finally, one morning with coolness in the air both camps began to get their things together and made the necessary preparations to move. They left everything as it was and headed south. When they got to Running Water Draw they made temporary camps as did Rob. The next morning both groups were headed downstream so Rob motioned to The Big Guy that he was going south. Each one of his group filed by and nodded as to say their good-byes and The New Guy also came over to acknowledge his departure. It was a little sad but Rob felt he had observed these people in most situations so he was anxious to experience possible new encounters and circumstances and compare this experience with what he had observed many of his years ago.

# Chapter 5

## New Directions

As the crow flies it was now only about 50 miles to his destination so there was no rush. He started to encounter some low sand hills from dry periods and the blowing sand northeast out of the Blackwater Draw drainage from the prevailing southwesterly winds. He saw quail, dove, prairie chickens and lots of smaller bird species, plus hawks, ravens and vultures. It was definitely a different biome. There were many low oak trees helping to stabilize the dunes and some larger ones in some of the more open areas. There were lots of tracks; horse, bison, antelope, deer and elk but all on the edge of the sand habitat. Since he had an adequate food supply and water he stayed on a direct course south across the dunes. It was tough going but in the deeper blowouts there were seep springs with a few cottonwoods and willows but lots of cattails, reeds and grasses. The water was good so he decided to spend the night at one. He made a depression above the spring on the northeast side of the dune. It was a clear night with a half moon and he had just dropped off to sleep when he was awakened by grunting and short squeals. It was unmistakably peccary. But they were under stress. Two adults and four young ones were milling around nervously. Then he saw the cause of their concern. A cat, not nearly as large as the lion he had seen some weeks before but certainly large enough to take down one of the peccary. The cat already had the advantage. His prey was caught between the water and steep sides of the dune. When they made a break for safety the cat cut off one of the younger ones and swiftly dispatched it. Rob had the slight breeze in his favor so he lay still and watched the predator eat most of the animal then covered the remainder with sand and peed on it. Fortunately, it departed the same way it came in. Since the cat had its fill Rob thought it would be OK to settle in for the rest of the night. He woke early and made his way to the top of the dune, as it turned out, one of the highest in the dune field. He could see the expanse of the Blackwater Draw valley and even down into the bottom in places. There were several large intermittent ponds. He saw a golden eagle circling, a badger topping out on another dune, a fox running on a flat below him and a mammoth. It IS a mammoth! Several of them, near one of the ponds. Geezee, they are big! Even at this distance he couldn't help but be overwhelmed. There they were, magnificent creatures, like elephants but bigger, and impressive beyond words. He watched them feed downstream for at least an hour. He wasn't sure what to do next. Get closer? Follow them? Were they aggressive toward all predators including and maybe especially, humans? He knew it would take multiple hunters with great skill to down one of these beasts. He decided to go down to where they had been and follow, at a safe distance of course. He will need to refurbish his food supply soon so he would also look for hunting and gathering opportunities. He was pretty sure he had come out a good ways upstream of the Blackwater Draw site that was discovered in the 20th century which was good. Very good, as he could survey other potential archaeological sites as he explored the draw and how and where it was being used by the Clovis people. There was only a small amount of flowing water from pond to pond but the ponds were large and appeared to be fairly deep. There were willows, cottonwoods, cattails and reeds. An occasional large oak intermingled with the dominant shrub oak that covered the sand hills. As he made his way downstream he realized that the ponds were a result of springs percolating out of the draw and then the overflow draining downstream. He didn't find any evidence of human occupation at this point but was sure he would encounter some sooner or later. He saw several small groups of deer, peccary and lots of rabbits. It wasn't hard to follow the mammoth trail because you could still smell them. Their droppings, feeding areas and tracks were obvious. He found a good camping spot near one of the ponds and set several rabbit snares and settled in. About dark he saw what appeared to be a large bobcat hunting the lower edge of the pond. But that wasn't enough to disturb his sleep that night. He had two rabbits the next morning and roasted both. There were lots of hoofed tracks coming in to the water so he set up to see if he could ambush whatever came next.

He woke up midmorning with a really bad headache and lots of flies buzzing around him. He felt blood on the back side of his head and heard voices. He had no clear picture of what had happened but it was becoming clear that someone had hit him hard with something really hard. He slowly sat up and tried to focus on the activities of those around him. One middle aged man was scolding a younger man and other men were observing them and Rob but not participating in the conversation. The older man came over and knelt down beside him looking at his wound but also looking him over. He showed no aggression or sympathy but went back to the younger man and chastised him some more. He directed two of the others to go over and help Rob up. He was a little wobbly but could navigate on his own. He then saw the short wooden baseball bat like club that the younger man was carrying which was most likely the weapon he had experienced first-hand. The two men helped him downstream while another one of the group picked up his belongings which he very much appreciated. They were camped only a few hundred yards from where he had been. Apparently the Village Idiot had discovered him while approaching the place where he was lying in wait for some game to come in. The bigger question was what did he fear from Rob? That was probably why the leader was dressing him down.

It was a fairly large encampment about 30 individuals. The Leader had two of the older women attend to Rob's cut. He had not been that close to any of the women previously and found they had an oily smell that was not unpleasant. They tended him quickly and well. They put an ointment on his head that did smell but he accepted the attention gratefully.

The Leader came over and said something to him but again Rob pointed to his ears and shook his head negatively. The Leader nodded and walked away saying something to the Village Idiot, which by the tone was not pleasant.

They offered him some fresh roasted meat which he ate gladly. It looked like they had been at that location a good while as there was a lot of jerky drying and half a dozen campfires established but this didn't appear to be, and he was pretty sure, that it was not the Blackwater Draw site that he was seeking. He saw no evidence of mammoth remains but lots of turtle carapaces of varying sizes. Their shelters were lean-toos like the previous ones he had encountered. The common denominator was the clothing and he had duplicated it pretty well.

There were quite a few more females than males in this group so it would stand to reason they would be doing some trading given the opportunity. It seemed a group consisting mostly of hunters and camp workers, in their child bearing years with an equal number of each being desirable. The two women who had attended to him came over and appeared satisfied with their medicinal skills. It was surprising that he didn't hurt that much. Some kind of numbing agent was in the mixture but no way of knowing what.

Rob took his material possessions and set up about 25 yards from the group. The Leader came over and motioned for him to follow. As he started to go with him and The Leader pointed at his belongs so he picked them up and followed him down to one of the shelters. He motioned for Rob to join one of the two women who had put the salve on his head. Rob wasn't quite sure what to do. She had probably lost her mate at some point and The Leader was probably arranging for her to take care of Rob and possibly make up for the Village Idiot's hasty attack on him. He decided the most appropriate thing to do would be to accept the accommodations so he put his stuff at the edge of the willow branch bed.

It was comfortable and fortunately the woman was already lying down with her back to him. She was either asleep or feigning sleep. He slept well after reflecting on all the events of the day and the journey, especially after coming in direct contact with even more Clovis people.

Milling activities and wood cracking awakened him. The woman had already joined the other older woman in preparing a meal. Five of the males, including the Village Idiot were preparing for a hunt. They all ate a mush from terrapin carapaces that may have been made from the prairie potato and tasted a little like oatmeal. Although he had a headache, Rob got his atlatl, darts, possibles bag and they headed downstream. They went past three large ponds and saw elk, deer and four-horned antelope but they were after something else. Maybe they were waiting on a fifth hunter to tackle a mammoth. Then he saw the prey. It was a mammoth! A female that had blood, both dried and fresh exiting a wound behind the shoulder but too low to inflict a fatal blow. She was aware of their presence immediately and turned to face them and made a false charge. The Village Idiot was the first to cast a dart. It went straight into the chest and looked like it had good penetration. The mammoth turned and Rob and all the rest of the hunters caste darts into the side of the animal. She fled downstream and as each got another dart ready and started to follow she stumbled and fell to her knees. They approached cautiously but it was obvious she was taking her last breath dying in a sudden death syndrome position kneeling with her head in an upright position. The Leader sent one of the younger men back upstream and another downstream. The Village Idiot was quite pleased with himself but The Leader said something to him and he became quite. Were they father and son? Had The Leader taken him in or just keeping him in line as the group's leader? By the time the women and a few children arrived the mammoth was dead. It took everyone to push the beast over so the butchering could begin. Rob's dart had ended up in a lung so once again he had lucked into looking good. As they were finishing the gutting process another band arrived from downstream. The butchering and sharing of the meat was definitely a communal event and probably the sharing would continue with other groups as there was more meat than could be consumed by these two tribal units before it ruined. Their efficiency was impressive. The men helped flesh out the choice pieces while the women made some willow travois and began to place the large pieces in layers sending some of the younger women back pulling what was close to 100 pounds each to their respective campsites. They were only able to get the top half of the animal butchered before everyone headed back.

Rob carried a large piece of back strap. He was as amazed as he was satisfied. He had been part of a mammoth kill! In this particular instance it was not a cultural statement or part of a religious event as some of his colleagues have postulated although it was very much a community affair. It was simply and specifically the result of a successful hunting venture. Had the cow still been with the herd they would not have been able to finish her off. His roommate had some roasted mammoth by the time he returned to the shelter. It was really good. She had added some salt and sage to it and it tasted like good beef. The sleeping arrangement was the same. She had her back to him and he was glad. The next morning some of the women and youngsters stayed behind to cut the slabs of meat into thin strips and put it on drying racks for jerky. The rest headed back to the kill site. The group from yesterday was already there cutting more meat from the bone. The two leaders got off to one side and had a conference.

Rob helped butcher the remaining hind quarter giving slabs to women from both groups. They continued until late afternoon when they stopped to eat some of the leftovers from last evening. Another group showed up from downstream. Someone from the previous day's clan must have known how to contact them. Everyone joined in and helped the new arrivals with their share. They worked until almost dark. The new group was preparing to stay at the kill site, which was probably dangerous considering the variety and number of large predators in the area.

Rob was really tired. The women had made the intestine soup. It was much stronger than what he had experienced previously, possibly because of what it was eating and because the animal had been under such stress after being wounded.

The next morning only a few of Rob's group returned to the kill site. When they got there several of the new group were looking at a dead animal near the mammoth. It was a sabertooth, but not a "tiger", its pelage was very similar to a mountain lion. Apparently the cat had tried to defend his portion and the men from the group killed the animal. They proceeded to skin it but they did not take anything but the hide. Maybe they had enough meat from the mammoth or the cat just wasn't desirable fare. They finished getting all the remaining meat off the bones by early afternoon and the third group packed up and headed downstream. It was not clear at this point whether they were going to use any of the bone and the tusks, although small, were still in place. Without question there would be other scavengers return to what the humans had left. Rob had decided he would remain a few more days then set out on his own again and try to find the Blackwater Draw site. Most of the activity revolved around the preparation of their winter storehouse. They did go back and get the top humerus and femur and brought them back to camp. They broke into the marrow which was shared by all. Rob was sure they would continue to use additional bone and ivory for tools, fore shafts and ornaments, but it was time to get to his objective as there was a chill in the air and with winter on the way he had to start making his way back to the Clovis Type Site. He could not miss the chance to get back to his other life and the opportunity to return to these places he had experienced.

He left his point he had recovered from the mammoth at the kill site under the skull. He gathered his belongings and went to The Leader and motioned he was leaving. The Leader acknowledged his intentions and said something to the woman with whom he had been sharing her shelter. She went to another shelter and brought back a beautifully tanned elk hide and offered it to Rob. He accepted with a bow and a nod. She smiled and The Leader nodded. Rob made it past the kill site and on down to the camp of the first group that had come to participate in the butchering. He didn't stop because he was sure The Leader had told their leader about his deafness. He continued on down the draw, found a small spring up a side channel and made camp. He was melancholy and suddenly felt lonely. A long, long way home, farthest anyone had ever been from home.

He got back on his way early and could have killed a peccary but was loaded with food. He didn't expect the next encounter, as he rounded a bend he saw a large lake not like the ponds he had been by before and a large encampment on the northeast side. He remembered his consternation as a grad student in surveying the northeast corner of the Blackwater Draw site and finding lots of flakes that had been bulldozed up as part of the Blackwater Draw gravel quarry operations.

There appeared to be some semi-permanent structures among the lean-too's with hide walls and tops but they still had four sides with an entry opening on what had become the front which generally faced southeast. It looked like there could be as many as 40 individuals and a dozen structures. He was pretty sure this was the origin of the third group to participate in the mammoth butchering. There were racks of jerky and lots of fresh meat being roasted.

He hoped their leader had learned of his deafness from The Leader but felt he should make his presence known. He approached the camp which caused a great deal of interest from the residents and a man he recognized came out to meet him and led him to a shelter which was one of those that looked permanent. There was a buffalo hide covering most of the floor. The man inside was dressed in finely tanned and sewn clothing. He had thicker beard than any of the other Paleo men thus far. He was probably between 35 and 40 years old. He had on an impressive necklace with various species of cat, canine claws, some eagle claws, shell beads and an ivory pendant. He was a stocky 5'7" or 8" tall. He motioned for Rob to sit and a middle-aged woman brought in drinks in two small gourds. He spoke briefly to the woman and she left. The drink tasted very blackberry and was the sweetest thing he had tasted since his teleportation. He appeared to be a medicine man and major player in the population. Rob felt welcomed in his presence. The Medicine Man did not speak but after a short time led him to a small brush shelter that was probably used for storage but had been hurriedly cleaned out for him. It likewise had a smaller bison hide covering the floor and a large gourd full of water. It wasn't quite the

Broadmoor but it sure was the best he had been in since coming back in time.

Rob had achieved his goal, almost. He had made it to the Blackwater Draw site and was now staying as a guest of the "chief" of the regional population of Paleo people. But he was only half way on his journey. He MUST get back to the Alibates Flint Quarry in time to catch his "ride" home. After a lot of contemplation he decided it would be best if he wintered as the Medicine Man's guest, at this first destination, if he was allowed to stay.

Even averaging only 5 miles a day it shouldn't take more than a month to get back to the quarry but he wouldn't take any chances. He would head back in March after spring had started to envelop the plains. In the meantime he would try to observe, comprehend and remember every part of their lives and livelihoods.

It started quickly, early the next morning he heard crying, multiple individuals, sobbing, and an emotion he had not experienced thus far. A young woman was carrying a child, clearly evident that it was deceased with several younger women behind her, obviously mourning the death of the child. It looked to be 2-3 years old but Rob couldn't determine sex or the cause of death. Several men were standing in the vicinity showing concern but not participating in the procession. The women took the deceased down to the water, undressed the boy, as it turned out, bathed the body and wrapped it in a tanned hide with short fur that looked to be a cat. They took him back to one of the semi-permanent shelters and the woman who was carrying the child sat in front of the opening. She would cut herself occasionally with a sharp flake and wail, but her mourning seemed somewhat subdued compared to what had been recorded by observers in frontier America. Maybe it was based on the longevity of the deceased or something related to the cultural mores of the period, he wasn't sure but he felt for the young woman.

People came to her and offered condolences and an occasional small gift, possibly a meaningful trinket or personal item in small pouches or gourds. The women began to make a funeral pyre with long sticks and limbs of mostly oak. They were going to cremate him! Makes sense, the need to properly dispose of the dead, quickly, so they wouldn't be dismembered or disgraced by predators or begin to decompose and be offensive to the survivors.

The women began to prepare a feast of sorts, combining efforts and food around a single campfire where everyone participated. The Medicine Man made a short soliloquy and chant and the mother lit the funeral pyre and it was over. Rob had witnessed a "burial" of sorts.

Life returned to normal over the next few days and he was invited to join a hunting party. Maybe The Leader had told the Medicine Man of his hunting success. They headed southwest around the lake to the edge of the draw. It was much steeper and provided better vantage points to get up on game from above. They passed on a couple of camels, but further up the draw they caught half a dozen deer making their way up from a pond and cut them off. Just as they topped out all five of the hunters cast their darts simultaneously. Rob's hit a doe a little far back but she went down about 50 yards away. Two of the other guys hit a buck, and it went down instantly. They made quick work of dressing out the animals and just like modern hunters tied them to poles and headed back to the encampment.

Rob guessed they thought he was too old to be on the end of the poles so they carried the game. He was OK with that and felt good about his continued ability, and luck, to contribute to the food supply.

The women took the kills and prepared the meat for distribution. They gave Rob a large piece of the back strap, which he took back to his shelter cutting it into smaller pieces and cooking part of it for the evening meal. He hung the rest on a rack he had built for jerky settling in and feeling good about his decision to overwinter here as it was getting colder. He was also glad for his elk hide and the gift hide but really needed some additional coverings for the summer shelter to block out the cold winds.

The next day he went on his on back upstream toward the mammoth kill wanting to see its condition after time and possibly bring down another animal for its hide.

He passed the camp where the second group had participated in butchering the mammoth but it had been abandoned, again with very little evidence of human occupation. Approaching the kill site cautiously to make sure there were no predators he discovered that most everything was gone. The remaining bones were scattered and the tusks were removed. The skull was still there but had a hole in the top where his former hosts had broken into it for the brain. The hide below the body was still there but there would be little evidence of human interaction.

He made his way up to the south rim of the draw. Almost immediately there was that sixth sense again that something was array, like he was being followed, maybe stalked. He did a slow 360 degree turn, but nothing evident. Then a second time, there it was, almost indistinguishable from the dead grass, a lion, either a large mountain lion or a young American lion. It was crouched, ready to spring or flee only about 15 yards awry, facing Rob, not a desirable shot but no choice. His only option was to cast a dart and either kill or scare him because he couldn't outrun him and he wouldn't have a second chance. He made his attempt quickly. The dart grazed the cat's side and apparently scared him. It took off like a rocket. Rob's knees went weak and he was shaking. He sat down and then lay down. Realizing the cat could come back he set out downstream. Passing the former campsite he saw some horses. He couldn't tell exactly how many as they were grazing among the brush and trees, but maybe a dozen. It would be almost impossible to get close enough for a shot from his location above them as they would see his approach so he decided to get back to camp and enlist some help.

As he approached the structures he almost didn't recognize his. They had covered it with hides in fact most of the others as well. It was starting to sleet with a snow mix so it was an easy decision not to go after the horses until the weather broke.

His domicile was most welcome and comfortable. He fixed some more venison and rested well. It was cold the next morning with snow covering the ground. The men were eating around a campfire and probably discussing where to hunt. Rob went up to them and pointed upstream. The other four got their gear together and he led the way. He chose to stay in the bottom as they would have a better chance of encountering and getting up on the herd without being detected. As they got close to where he had seen them the day before, they found fresh tracks. The hunters spread out and made their way forward slowly. He heard hoof beats. One or two of the other guys had hit one of the horses and they had bolted. The hunters followed. They should have backed off and let the animal hold up to bleed out but they kept pushing. In the long run it worked and they finally caught up with the young stallion. It was still standing but in desperate straits. One of the hunters who had hit him finished him off. They quartered him and Rob carried the hide with each of the others carrying a boned out quarter. It was dark and spitting snow by the time they got back. He spread the hide out in the snow and went to bed very tired.

The women brought him another chunk of back strap the next morning. He roasted some and found it to be very good. He continued to mark his staff daily and realized it was his birthday. He would never in his wildest imagination have thought he would be in a hut at Black Water Draw 13,000 years removed from Colorado and Della on his 70th observance. Sometimes his situation hit him hard.

It was cold and the wind was blowing. It was a good day to stay inside. He ate some jerky and some of his version of trail mix. Apparently Medicine Man was concerned about his welfare, as he and The Young Woman who had lost her child came over to bring him some of the blackberry tasting drink and some stew probably from the horse. It was all good and unbeknown to them a great birthday present. Medicine Man left but The Young Woman stayed.

Rob didn't know why or if there were multiple reasons. Medicine Man was smart, contemplative and had meaningful reasons for his actions. She may be a gift for what he had contributed to the group or his desire to see Rob's genes passed on since he had lived so long. Maybe she had lost her mate and needed a companion or possibly all of these scenarios played a part in his decision. In any event Rob was again in a difficult position. She busied herself cleaning the eating and drinking gourds along with the turtle carapaces. She had on a beautifully tanned elk dress but the moccasins were like the other he had seen made from much tougher hides like bison or peccary. She had brought with her a nice robe from something he had not encountered. Maybe musk ox, had they been further north or was it a trade item? The Young Woman wore a necklace with mostly beads of shell and ivory but also a very large lion claw. Was that what killed her mate or was that from a suitor? She said something but he couldn't tell if she was talking to him or to herself. He pointed to his ears and shook his head negatively, she acknowledged positively. She had long reddish brown hair and was not unattractive especially compared to the older women who had experienced hard lives for a longer period.

She began to drop some of the hot stones surrounding the small fire into the largest of the turtle carapaces. She took a tanned piece of hide out of her possibles bag and a root. Rob recognized it as yucca. Over 50 years earlier in his other life he remembered a neighbor who continued to use yucca as a shampoo long after the proliferation of commercial hair products became popular. She had him lie down and she began to wash his hair. It was now shoulder length and it was mostly white like his beard. It was extremely satisfying and relaxing. She dried it with the soft shammy-like hide she had gotten from her bag. She wrapped the ox fur robe around him and that was all he needed to fall asleep. He was aware she had wrapped herself in his elk hide and put her back to his. He woke briefly during the night and like all old men had to pee.

But came back and assumed the same position with much apprehension about what the immediate future held for both of them.

The next morning he woke up to find her fixing a soup with some of the small squash, herbs and some dried fish. It was excellent. These people were beyond crafty. They were quite sophisticated and resourceful utilizing their environment far better than he and his colleagues could ever have imagined.

It was clear but very cold and he decided to pay a visit to The Medicine Man. The snow crunched under foot on his way over. He continued to use the ox robe and The Medicine Man pointed to it smiled and nodded. He responded likewise. Rob pointed to his groin and held out his index finger straight then let it curl downward. The Medicine Man caught on instantly and put a hand on his shoulder and nodded affirmatively. The Medicine Man wrapped a buffalo robe around him and they went back to Rob's structure. As they entered the Medicine Man spoke to The Young Woman and she nodded with no change in her expression. The Medicine Man once again put his hand on Rob's shoulder and nodded. Rob simply bowed his head and the Medicine Man left. Rob had read somewhere that in a survey of modern women over 50% preferred snuggling to sex after a certain age. He hoped that would be the case with The Young Woman. He also hoped he could control his instincts but that might not be a problem since he had not had his prostate medicine since arriving here and it would probably make his lack of abilities noticeable.

That night he lay on his back and she snuggled against him and they fell asleep. That became the routine. On fall like days they took walks together and became close friends even without speaking. Her powers of observation were exceptional, seeing and pointing out the small things that even good hunters miss. She was with him when he killed a peccary and took over the cleaning and butchering process. He couldn't understand why some of the young men were not interested in her except for the possibility she was her own person and might not be as submissive as the other women. Whether she saw Rob as a father figure or just simply as someone who respected her as an equal really didn't matter. They made the relationship work.

Rob remembered Thanksgiving although not the exact date but did reflect on all his blessings both in the real world as well as this one. The group didn't seem to be aware of and certainly didn't celebrate the winter solstice. However, he did know when it was Christmas and became very depressed. He was sure Della was too, not knowing if he was alive or even if she would see him in four more months. He wished he could have some way to let them know he was ready to go back.

By the first part of January it was obvious the food supply was getting low. So the usual five headed south into the Llano Estacado with its playas and draws. Game was scarce, probably much further south, but they did encounter some four-horned antelope which proved to be much too wary and they never got close enough for a shot. They spent a cold clear night on the trail and headed west. The Caprock was not nearly as prominent at this latitude but still provided a vantage point and they could see some bison at a large lakebed about a mile away. The others discussed strategy and headed southwest in order to come into the north wind. Once they got close they flushed a large bunch of prairie chickens as they got to level ground but they flew south with the wind so probably didn't alarm the bison. One of the men grabbed Rob by the arm and motioned that they wanted to take only the smaller ones, Rob nodded affirmatively. As they got closer Rob thought he recognized the lake as one he had surveyed as a grad student. He remembered a fairly deep ravine running into it on the southwest corner. He broke away from the group as they moved forward. His ploy worked as the other four cast their darts at their prey half a dozen bison came charging up the ravine. Two yearlings were to-gether and he cast a dart as they went past. They were only about 10 yards away but slightly below him. He didn't hit the first one but caught the second one in the neck. Blood started spurting out. It had got the juggler! He couldn't believe his luck, again. He was just trying to hit some part of either one. It didn't make it to the top of the lake bed. The other guys had also killed one. They boned out the meat and tied hunks together and between them were able to take most of the best parts of the two animals back.

They seemed surprised that Rob could carry his share. By cutting straight across they were able to make it back to camp shortly after dark. The Young Woman hugged Rob upon his return and took the meat from him. She began to prepare some of it for preserving and sharing. He had put what he was car-rying in one of the back hides and she staked it out working by the half moon and the stars. It was hard to comprehend how bright they were on a clear winter's night. She snuggled very close after they finally got to bed. They were both very tired but he was afraid he would have an erotic dream or she would see an early morning, "got to pee" erection. But she never indicated anything other than the desire to take care of him. They seemed to have an admiration for each other's abilities, intelligence and curiosity. She was a superb hunter of small game, rabbits especially and once speared a prairie chicken. They were not as wild as the ones he had hunted on the plains of Colorado acting much like a Blue Grouse in the mountains, but it was still no easy task.

As the days got longer and winter loosened its grip on the landscape the group seemed to have a new energy and hunters were going out in pairs. They brought in lots of yearling bison, horses and antelope. Like other predators they were taking advantage of last year's crop which suffered most from the winters.

One morning a pack of wolves appeared on the south side of the lake and almost as choreographed everyone charged them hollering and shouting needless to say the canines turned tail and raced out of sight quickly. That strategy certainly left an impression on each individual in the pack that humans probably should be avoided.

Toward the end of February one of the hunters came and got Rob. He pointed to the ridgeline above the lake. A bachelor herd of mammoths were making their way up the draw. The hunters and young boys were watching and talking among themselves discussing the challenges of encountering what would probably be a very aggressive and dangerous prey. The hunter who had come to get Rob came over to him and pointed at the herd. Rob in no way wanted to take a chance of getting hurt or maybe killed at this point in his incredible journey and shook his head negatively. The hunter turned and said something to the group. They watched as the animals went out of sight. As Rob turned to go back to his shelter The Medicine Man was standing close by and nodded approvingly.

# Chapter 6

# Companions

It was getting close to the time for him to head back toward the quarry. He had not yet indicated to The Young Woman that he would be leaving and felt he needed some reinforcement. He went to The Medicine Man and pointed to himself and then pointed north. The Medicine Man nodded accepting his decision. Rob then pointed to his shelter where The Woman was working outside and shook his head negatively. The Medicine Man looked surprised then grim and after a few long moments acknowledged his intentions.

As The Medicine Man went back with him to his lodge and began to explain the circumstances to The Young Woman. Her reaction was immediate and firm shaking her head negatively. The Medicine Man tried to reason with her but there was a determination in her response that could not be ignored. The Medicine Man turned to Rob and put his hands out and shrugged – a clear message that he could do no more and walked away. She was obviously upset with Rob and didn't acknowledge his presence for the rest of the day.

He began to accept her going with him but it certainly complicated things in his eventual departure. He would really have to plan it so she wouldn't experience his sudden disappearance. He went over to her after their evening meal and hugged her. She hugged him back hard, understanding that she would be going with him.

During the next few days they made preparations for their journey. She didn't seem upset that she was leaving the group, in fact seemed to be looking forward to the adventure that lay ahead of them.

When the morning came for them to leave the whole group came out to see them off. This time The Young Woman and Rob walked along the line and nodded their good byes. The Medicine Man positioned himself last. He stood erect and looked at each of them a long time. He must have had some personal, familial connection with The Young Woman. He put a necklace around Rob's neck. It was simple but magnificent. It only had a single, possibly matching, lion claw to the other one that The Young Woman wore. Rob bowed his head in thanks. Maybe it was The Medicine Man's son who had been killed.

They headed northeast into a fresh spring breeze loaded with food and water turning back to look when they got to the edge of the draw. The camp had returned to its daily cycle and they looked at each other and she hugged him. They made good time encountering only a few ridges of sand hills and were then back on the Llano Estacado. He so much wanted to divert to the Lubbock Lake but he couldn't take the chance of losing control of the time remaining to meet his destiny for this life

They made a good 15 miles the first day and camped on a small rise close to where Clovis, New Mexico and the Texas state line is in the present day. Four-horned antelope and coyotes and deer were plentiful but they had as much food as they could carry at this point. The Young Woman fixed some fresh roasted bison and some of the small squash which she baked in the ground at the edge of the fire. Everything was good.

They made it to Running Water Draw the next day but didn't come out at one of the ponds so they camped by the stream in a large grove of pecan trees. They gathered a large number of the nuts from the previous fall. There had been deer and peccary feeding on them as well and staying there the next day hulling the nuts to add to their "larder" was very rewarding.

What happened to these people leaving no genetic trace in the Native American linage? These immigrants were certainly well equipped physically and mentally to survive. A question he would not be able to answer even with all the information he would be taking back.

It was fortuitous that she indicated she wanted to stay there a little longer. She was having her period and it was their custom she had to be alone. So Rob was able to retrace almost every footstep in his mind to better secure the memories of his own entrada and rest his aging body. His old arthritic joints were aching and his hemorrhoids were becoming more pronounced. Some of the places on his face and ears were getting "crusty." The doctors were going to have their hands full when he did get back.

The next day he followed The Young Woman's tracks to where she had made a makeshift brush shelter, tipi in shape and had built a small fire and created a quick sweat lodge. He backed off without her knowing he had been there when he saw she was OK. She returned the next morning and bathed in the stream. It was all he could do not to pursue the opportunity to have sex with her. They gathered their things and continued on a northeasterly course. They made it to Frio Draw by late afternoon and it was running full. Much too fast and wide to cross at this point, they would have to make their way upstream to find a safe crossing. They camped at a vantage point where they could see all around them. He realized they were getting close to where he and the first band he stayed with had camped although they were still downstream from there. He also realized she was getting tired and decided they would spend a few days at the old encampment for her to rest.

The stream was getting narrower but still running fast and at an unknown depth. They ate jerky and their rendition of trail mix and kept moving until they got to the camp site. The stream was crossable there and he quickly made a brush shelter from what had been left previously. It was much cooler in the bottom of the draw so he built the fire and set a couple of snares outside her sight. He caught a rabbit fairly quickly and took it back and roasted it. She seemed very appreciative that he was willing to fix the meal. He put some of the nuts in a small gourd and brought her some fresh water. She fell asleep early and they stayed there three days while he took care of her for a change.

She was feeling much better as they struck out again. This time a little more easterly but still on a course that would take them to the crossing on the Palo Duro where he first met The Big Guy and his band. Since they had to go so far to the west they were a good 60 miles away from that crossing. They took their time resting a little more often. They had been lucky, the spring showers had held off and it was still not too hot, in fact most pleasant.

They were able to find the well-worn trail on the fifth day and followed it to the crossing by late that afternoon. There had been an encampment there recently and he was guessing it was one of the groups he had encountered or one from Lubbock Lake headed north.

Now he wished he was younger and NASA could retrieve him on command so he could follow these people to their summer destination. By his accounting it was April 10 the day before his best friend's birthday and probably the first time he had not sent him a greeting in over 60 years. He guessed there would be some media coverage when he got back and John would know why then.

He led the way up the draw to the shelter and did not see any wolf or lion tracks. The Young Woman seemed pleased and nodded positively. She started to settle in and he went upstream to make sure there were no surprises in store. Everything seemed to be in order and he started back. He saw a young buck deer making his way toward him. It was on alert but had not seen Rob. He stopped behind a tree and got ready to take a shot. The deer never turned sideways to him so his only option was a front on attempt. He missed and broke his point in the process. He took the dart, fore shaft and base back to the shelter to show The Young Woman and shook his head negatively. She patted his arm and gave him the, "it's OK look." She was already fixing a meal of stew from several of the items remaining in the knapsack. As usual it was good and he recounted how he had missed the deer with sign language. She laughed and they enjoyed each other's company and rested well.

They had a month to get the last 60 miles so it would be most pleasant to stay here a while. He did kill a deer, caught several rabbits and they had a good respite. They once again had plenty of food and water to make the last leg of his journey. He worried about what she would do when he was translocated. But he knew she was a strong woman and without a doubt knew where the groups were headed on their northern trek, in fact, she was probably ahead of some of them at this juncture. The last part of the trip was through the Canadian River breaks which were rough going. They averaged about 10 miles a day and camped at the head of the draws. He could tell she was getting tired again. They were close to his original shelter. He took her sleeping hides and carried them for her.

They had to wade across a wide part of the Canadian where it was shallower as the spring rains had begun in earnest. He made a fire from the wood he had left in the shelter and helped her take off her dress so he could put it between the fire and the back wall of the shelter to dry and put the ox robe around her. Rob was also wet and cold but he toughed it out drying himself close to the fire.

He could tell she had lost weight. The trip had been long and hard but he had the feeling she was glad she had come with him. He worried even more about her loneliness after he was gone. Maybe she knew instinctively that this was his last journey and was preparing herself for his demise. They had made a good team and would remember each other for the rest of their lives. She had a chill and he held her closely that night but she was up early making the blackberry tea from the concoctions in her little bag of spices, salt and whatever else. It was delightful and they both enjoyed it and their time together. He set out to find the stake he had left in the ground. When she started to follow he motioned for her to stay. She did but with obvious reluctance. He was pretty sure she would follow anyway and that was OK until the last day.

By his calculations it was May 1st. He had met the challenge, actually many challenges, and made it back in time. It had been an extraordinary opportunity to live with the Paleo people of the Americas and it was hard to believe it had happened to him.

As he got to the hill he noticed some smoke coming from below the quarry. It was quite a bit further down the River but on the same side they were on. Had the knapper survived the torrent? At least someone was staying here. He started to put some large stones in a circle around the stake. He wasn't sure why? Maybe to make it more meaningful for The Young Woman. He sat down in the middle looking down at the stake and his future. What had happened while he was gone? Was everything still a "go"? He would know soon enough.

He sat there a good while contemplating how he would make sure no one saw his instantaneous removal from this time period. At least it would be night but no one knew what retrieval looked like to anyone that might be observing the occurrence.

He headed back to the shelter and could tell from the tracks she had followed him to a point where she could see him making the stone circle. He was glad. That may help her accept the inevitable. She acted as if nothing was amiss and fixed their evening meal.

He had to leave her with some meat and planned to do some hunting over the next few days. He started out early the next morning but turned around and came back. He took her to the circle and pointed to the other shelter and motioned with seriousness that was a danger. She acknowledged and they went back to the shelter. She hugged him hard. He motioned for her to get her atlatl and darts and come with him, she was pleased.

They went upstream. The river was swollen and there were storm clouds already building in the west. They got on the rim and made their way along slowly looking for game. All at once they heard what sounded like an animal screaming. It took a minute to comprehend what they were seeing. It was a baby mammoth in the river in its last throws of trying to stay afloat. The mother or the rest of the herd were not in sight so it must have been in the water for a long time and was going past them at a rapid rate.

He remembered where he had found the bison in the sharp bend in the river. He motioned for The Young Woman to follow quickly. They passed their shelter and sure enough the baby was caught up in the same log jam. It was dead but how do they get to him and then get him out of the river? They sat down on the bank and looked at each other. Rob shrugged and she looked at him as if to say, "I don't know either."

The water was cold so it would be OK even for a few days. Maybe the water would recede enough for them to cross and butcher it. They went back to the shelter exhausted. They ate jerky and trail mix and fell asleep early. They could not count on retrieving the mammoth. So they set out again to see if they could get some more meat. They went northwest into some wooded drainages and found lots of game, but very few opportunities to get close enough for a shot. Finally, they found a bachelor herd of whitetail bucks making their way up a draw toward them. They were feeding so they were moving slowly. Rob got behind one tree and The Young Woman behind another and waited on the deer to pass by. The wind was in their favor and the draw was wide enough that they weren't too close to the game. Rob felt they should take the first one coming through as there would be more eyes and ears if they waited. They got ready and cast their darts at the same time. Both darts hit the animal but hers was much better placed. He guessed he was just getting old!

They worked together and had it ready to carry back to camp in a few minutes. She placed the heart and liver inside the body cavity and got on the other end of the pole. Rob was amazed at her strength. They had to stop a few times to rest on the way back which was just as welcome to him as it was to her. They skinned it out, hung the quarters and had fresh heart and liver that night. They were both greatly satisfied with each other's efforts.

She had already staked out the skin by the time he got up the next morning and was roasting some back strap. It was amazing how these people could adapt to whatever conditions they encountered, positive or negative.

He went down to the bend in the river to see what was happening. The river was coming down but still too dangerous to attempt to cross. He went back up to his circle and sat there for a while. He was pretty sure he could hear some knapping. So the guy survived, he was glad, that gave him an idea, as soon as he could cross over to the mammoth he could tie a rope on it and come back across, stake out the rope and maybe the 3 of them could pull it loose and let it float downstream to their side of the river. All he had to do was make a rope, fashion a big stake and enlist the knapper. There would be plenty of meat for all of them.

He figured the green hide would be best if he cut it in wide enough strips to connect the length which would also make it stronger. He found a large oak limb on his side at the bend and fashioned it to a point. He spent the rest of the day getting everything ready. He showed The Young Woman his plan but could tell she didn't understand the thought process.

The next morning he was pretty sure he could get across the river so he went to find The Knapper. He sensed that The Young Woman was following him which was OK as long as she stayed out of sight.

He followed the sound of the knapping and circled a little to come toward him so he would see he wasn't carrying his atlatl and darts. To say The Knapper was taken by surprise would be a gross understatement. He jumped up and reeled backwards. He grabbed his atlatl and a dart and before Rob had a chance to motion that he was unarmed he let it fly. Rob dodged but not quite quickly enough and the point struck him a glancing blow in the left upper arm but it inflicted a major wound. The Young Woman saw this and came running toward them yelling something. That also took The Knapper aback. Whatever she said made him drop his weapon and look stunned. Rob was on the ground bleeding profusely. It hadn't cut an artery but it was deep. The Young Woman ran over to him and tore off some of the sleeve on her dress and held it tightly around his arm. She obviously had done this before because she quickly picked up a large flake and split one end and tied the bandage even tighter. He could tell that it was going to stop the bleeding.

She went over to The Knapper and gave him a short but firm lecture. He hung his head and nodded positively. She went back over to Rob, checked the bandage and helped him up. Rob went over to The Knapper and motioned for him to follow. The Young Woman gave Rob a dirty look, tugged on his good arm as if to say, "What the hell do you think you are doing?" Rob just patted her hand.

The Knapper was like a whipped puppy and dutifully followed. They got to the bend and he showed The Knapper the baby mammoth. The Knapper's eyes lit up. Rob then showed him the "rope" he had made tied to the stake. He had The Young Woman interpret for him. He picked up the loose end, made a swimming motion, demonstrated tying the rope on the mammoth, swimming back and the three of them pulling the body from the log jam and letting it float downstream to their side of the river.

He could tell The Knapper was following the scenario and snatched the rope from Rob jumped in and swam to the mammoth! The Knapper pointed to the most exposed rear leg and Rob shook his head "yes". He swam back and although Rob could only use his right arm they all got on the rope and pulled. It eased out a little and Rob pulled hard again. They all tried again together. The mammoth came loose and the water carried it down swiftly. When it hit the end of the make-shift rope it almost pulled the stake out, but they rushed down and the three of them were able to get the animal up far enough on the bank that they could butcher it.

They were all elated and The Knapper was slapping Rob on the back until The Young Woman stopped him. The Knapper told The Woman something and headed back to the quarry. She motioned for Rob to stay where he was and went back to their shelter and got her small bag of salve. She carefully untied the bandage and put some on the cut and retied it.

The Knapper returned with some freshly made knives and they began the process. Rob wasn't much help except in holding the legs while they dismembered the animal. The stomach hide was much thinner but would make good moccasins.

They hauled their "catch" up the bank and The Knapper began apologizing to The Young Woman. Rob could tell that he had some disability in speaking possibility from the injury to his head and probably he was able to be useful to the population by doing one thing well, and that was knapping. Rob pointed to himself and shook his head affirmatively. He was trying to say he was OK. That brought tears to The Young Woman's eyes and she said something else to The Knapper and he cried.

These were extremely sensitive and good people with the same feelings all humans share. Hopefully, "moderns" have not strayed too far from their roots, these pre-historic roots.

The Knapper took a quarter and headed for his camp. Rob took the rope off of what was remaining of the carcass and kicked into the river. They watched it being carried downstream so it wouldn't attract predators to their shelter.

Rob and The Young Woman together were able to get a quarter back to their shelter and she began cutting it up. Rob lay down as he felt a little out of it. He had only a couple more days and…

He woke with The Young Woman putting cold soft hide on his forehead. He had a fever. It was mid-morning but which day?! How long had he been out?

The mammoth quarter had been cut up, but she was good at that so it could have been done quickly. He looked around and didn't see the other quarter but she couldn't have dragged it up to the shelter by herself.

He tried to find a way to ask her how long he had been asleep but she wouldn't let him get up. At least he had the rest of the day to recoup and think. He needed to determine if he should get ready to go that night. She fixed him a broth from the mammoth. It tasted like beef and he ate it with gusto and felt better.

He was weak but decided he couldn't risk not being in place just in case he was out for two days and not just one. He waited until she fell asleep. It was dark but he knew the trail and there was some ambient star light. He got to the circle probably around 8 pm. He sat down in the circle. He was better but still didn't feel well. He kept nodding off and about two hours later headed back to the shelter. He crawled into bed and held her trying to express his appreciation for being his partner through this part of his journey and life.

The next morning she fixed him some more broth which he welcomed. He went through his belongings making sure she would know what everything was and its usefulness. He was satisfied she would. He also placed the neckless that the Medicine Man had given him in his possibles bag for her to have as a memento of their time together.

They brought up their other quarter. The Knapper had already been back and retrieved his. She fixed some of the trunk for the evening meal and it was the best yet. He went over to her as she was cleaning up and held her tightly. She began to cry. He kissed her on the forehead then kissed the tears away and she kissed him longingly. They held each other for a long time.

He started up the trail and looked back and shook his head very firmly "no" and she nodded reluctantly but affirmatively. He got to the spot before 8 PM, pulled up the stake and sat down where it had been. He was very tired but his thoughts were keeping him alert. What if he ran down to the mammoth remains and covered his hand with blood. He could take the DNA back with him. But he was never convinced that cloning an extinct organism was a good idea. It would be profitable for sure, but not for the animal. He found himself tearing up because he was leaving with many questions still unanswered. Many observations that would be helpful to the field but mostly concern for The Young Woman. She had become very special to him and he wanted her to have a long and fruitful life…Maybe…

# Chapter 7

# Back

**S**uddenly he felt that he had been given anesthesia and was a little dazed. He was sitting on the floor of the "center". Several clinically covered people rushed to him, began to take swabs from various parts of his body, sticking them into tubes and capping them quickly. Then they began to wipe him down with the antiseptic which stung like hell on his cut.

They brought him out to a shower and he relished the warm water and soap. They had his favorite jeans, tee shirt, shorts and shirt for him to put on. Only Della would have known to bring those items. His drop kit was there but all he used was the deodorant for now. They took pictures of him in his shorts from several angles.

Dr. Baker met him in the first room and began to check him over. "How did you get the cut?"

Long story, I'll tell you about it later.

How long ago?

3 or 4 days.

Too late for stitches we'll just butterfly it but there will be a bad scar.

It will help me remember.

Any other bad places?

Rob pointed to the back of his head.

Wow! That was quite a blow.

Tell me about it!

No, I want YOU to tell me about it.

Later.

OK, you seem to be OK. We'll do a complete going over tomorrow.

OK

I'll send in antiseptic and a butterfly patch.

OK, alright already.

With that done Dr. Ellis came in and congratulated him on the successful venture.

It was a team effort but you made it back.

Rob was appreciative of the accolades but didn't know or understand why he was being so angry and defensive. As he started down the hallway the Colonel and the General approached to welcome him back.

The General was brief. "The Colonel will take you to the guest quarters where your wife is."

That was the only thing Rob wanted to hear.

The Colonel went over an agenda but he paid little attention to it except "You can spend tomorrow morning with your wife." Rob just said, "Thanks". When they got to the room Della let him in and they held each other for a long time. He couldn't hold back his tears and she was crying too. She expressed concern over the bandage on his arm, how much weight he had lost and what all he had been through but said he could tell her about everything later.

She was prepared to just hold him all night but he was more than ready to make love to her. She was glad. They fell asleep holding each other. She woke first and ordered breakfast. He woke when they delivered it. They ate and she asked if he had sex with any of those Paleo women and he said, "No", and that was all that was discussed about that part of his year away from her. She said it had been a long lonely year, she had missed his companionship. He told her he had thought about her every day. He wanted to get a barber, have his beard shaved off and get a really short haircut but Della talked him out of it.

"Just a trim all the way around and keep your good looks." She knew what was best in that regard. She went over to the phone and called a barber.

They said, "Anything you need or want."

The barber, with Della's direction and inspection, finished his efforts about 8:30 am.

NASA had left Della with an agenda and Rob ran through it quickly:

9 – 10am – Complete physical and psychological exams with Dr. Baker and Dr. Thomas Wiley

10:00 – Noon – Begin debriefing with General Woodward , Colonel Mathis, Dr. Baker, Dr. Ellis, Dr. Wiley including initial meetings with Dr. Ross, Dr. Anderson and Dr. Leftwich as time allows

Noon – Lunch with the Teleportation Crew with approximately 100 in attendance. Dr. Roby will be expected to make a few remarks

2PM – News Conference – All major networks and media representatives are expected to attend

The next meeting with colleagues will be the following morning at 8AM breakfast.

Rob – to himself but out loud, "News Conference? "I'm not ready to hold a news conference! I mostly need to be alone to debrief myself. I need to meet with the psychiatrist FIRST... RIGHT NOW!"

Before he had to face all of the scheduled events. He knew NASA had to make the most of their and his successful translocation, BUT, he needed some time to transport himself back to this time period.

He called Colonel Mathis and expressed his now desperate concern about his anxiety and need to meet with Dr. Wiley before anything else happens. The Colonel said he would call him right back. The Colonel called within five minutes and said that Ferguson would pick him up and take him to Dr. Wiley's office in 10 minutes. Della was listening and asked if he wanted her to go along with him. He held her and said that this was the last thing he needed to do alone but wanted her to be at all the other events they would allow her to attend.

I want you to be my present memory because I am overwhelmed at this point and I need to remember what I say to whom.

Of course, I understand and will be there with you.

I'll ask that you be allowed to accompany me to everything and I'll call you as soon as I find out.

I'll be here.

The phone rings and it is young Ferguson. Rob meets him in the lobby and asks him to see if it would be OK for Della to sit in on the various meetings and let her know and he said he would. They arrived at Dr. Wiley's office a little before 9 AM.

Come in Rob. I called Dr. Baker and told him I have you first.

Thanks Doc, I appreciate getting a chance to talk to you before I have to face all of – "This", making the quote motion with his fingers.

Tell me your concerns.

Why am I so defensive, if not angry?

You have been through something no one else has ever experienced and no one can fully understand. You are trying to tie the two worlds together and it cannot happen overnight. For what it's worth, I recommended a week of de-compression before we announced you were safely back. But they were afraid of a leak and they wouldn't be able to control the outcome.

I understand that but how can you help me pull this off?

You are definitely in a difficult position but from our first visit I was im-pressed with your mental strength and that's why I recommended you without question.

Pause.....

So you have to dig deep and put your most recent encounters in perspec-tive. That is, you will never forget them, but you will never be able to go back to that life. You need to come back to this world and think about what everyone wants to know. What was it like? How did you survive? Who did you en-counter? Where did you go and when were you there? AND why did you want to do this?

Seems simple when you put the questions to it.

I think if you concentrate on peoples' curiosity and how you would answer, say, to your wife, those questions you will be fine.

Thanks Doc, this has been, you have been, most helpful. I believe I can handle this now.

You can, and I'm glad I could help you look at the circumstances and chal-lenges a little differently perhaps.

You have pulled my rear out of the fire and I appreciate it.

I'll get Ferguson to take you over to Dr. Baker's office.

Just a minute Doc – pause – we are in the confidential mode aren't we – that is you – what I tell you is between us isn't it?

Yes, of course.

I am extremely concerned about someone I left behind and I feel guilty about abandoning her – pause – if it hadn't been for her I probably wouldn't have made it back.

I take it you had a close bond with her.

78

Yes, but not sexual, but very close.

Did you tell her you would be leaving?

Yes, in a way that she understood I'm sure.

Was she in danger?

I don't believe so, no more than she would normally face during that time period.

Did she have ample provisions to survive?

Yes, and she was a good hunter.

Do you feel you did all you could to help her face her future?

Yes, I supposed so, but...

You are going to experience some, if not a great deal, of separation anxiety, not unlike losing a mate. It's alright to grieve for the loss. So, concentrate on the good times and give it some well-deserved time to heal. Rest assured you did all you could to make sure she would be OK.

Thanks again Doc, I am deeply appreciative.

Ferguson takes Rob over to Baker's office where he gets a complete physical. He told the doctor about how he received his injuries and got appointments with the dentist and dermatologist. The doctor ordered some new prostate medicine and would possibly order something for joint relief after they got the blood work back.

They barely had time to get to the conference room in the General's office. There were greetings all around but especially glad to see him were Mike, Harry and Bill. Della was there too! The debriefing actually went well.

He found himself talking directly and mostly to his three colleagues and Della. He told them exactly where he went and the people he met, his hunting successes, the environment he encountered, including the weather, as well as the flora and fauna. Everyone got caught up in his excitement about his experiences and there was very little time for their questions before they went to the Center for the luncheon.

It was a little scary with him and Della at the head table with the General and Colonel and Dr. Ellis, although that went well too. He thanked everyone for their support and knowledge about how to get him there AND back. He made a joke about someone having his "remains" in a jar on their desk. It ended by the group giving him a standing ovation.

There was a little time before the news conference. The General and Colonel told him how proud they were that he had been their choice and how well he was handling everything with just a night's rest. They also apologized for not giving him more time to decipher his thoughts about his journey before they held theses events. He assured them they had done the right thing and that everything was OK from his end. He and Della stayed at the head table and had another cup of glorious coffee and he had another piece of pie.

Well over a 100 media people showed up where they had held the luncheon. Some were trying to get to him before the event officially got underway but the NASA protective service personnel kept them back. The General, the Colonel and Dr. Ellis came back in and the General made short introductions and directed everyone's attention to the large monitor. The President came on live to welcome Rob back and congratulated him on the successful Teleportation and said how much he appreciated the staff at NASA for this monumental accomplishment and that he was looking forward to a full report. He ended by saying, "as much as Jefferson looked forward to Lewis and Clark's account of their travels."

The Colonel gave a brief background of the project and how Rob was selected. Dr. Ellis tried to simplify how the process worked and how they had a known limited window in which to accomplish the teleportation. Then the General introduced Rob. Rob made a few general comments on why he wanted to go back to this particular time period and what his objectives were.

Questions?

Where did all this take place?

Did you actually see and interact with these people?

What did they look like?

Did you see a mammoth?

Did you kill one?

What other animals did you see?

What was the weather like?

Were you injured?

What did you eat?

Would you go back?

Did you make some friends?

How were the women and children treated?

He answered each question with patience in detail and finally –

How would you summarize your experience?

It was an incredible journey and I want to thank everyone here at NASA for the opportunity and my colleagues who helped me get prepared for the journey. I was able to enter another very different world, but the people were just like us, not necessarily in appearance, but I found them to be just as creative, if not as innovative in their technology as we are in ours. We just have the advantage of 13,000 years of cumulative knowledge. They were a lot more adaptable than we are. They were able to survive without all of our modern conveniences in extremely hostile surroundings. They have the same feelings, sadness, joy, love, fears and sense of pride in accomplishment that we do and while I didn't find out what happened to them I hope I – we have paved the way for the next voyager to discover what did. We have come a long way with different forms and stages of advancement, but have we lost some of our humanity? Have we lost respect and care for one another? Along with all of our achievements have we also built our egos so we are no longer willing to accept and understand others' looks, ideas, beliefs and ways of life or is everyone and everything a threat to our individual islands? The people I met were refreshingly simple, honest, industrious and cooperative. That's what made their society work. If we are as advanced as we think, then we should be able to develop a culture that our forefathers believed would accommodate all of its citizens and would afford progress with harmony. Idealistic, admittedly, but you asked what I brought back and that was my most lasting impression.

One of the reporters started clapping then the whole assemblage joined in.

The General stepped up and thanked everyone for coming and offered NASA's services to arrange for individual interviews with Rob. Rob and Della just looked at each other questioningly. Geezee, wasn't this enough?! Apparently not! The General and Colonel shook Rob's hand and thanked him for his observations and comments and assured him that they wouldn't schedule any interviews without his approval. Rob asked if he and Della could go back to their room. The General called Ferguson over and they left. Rob wanted and needed to rest. Della told him how proud she was of him and how glad she was to be a part of "their" adventure.

Rob slept until late evening. Della had not eaten either so he ordered barbeque and Louisiana crawfish etouffe, pintos, potato salad and cobbler. They ate until they were miserable. He watched the news on TV and Della filled him in on the many things that had happened while he was gone. They fell asleep holding each other. He awoke early and got ready to meet with colleagues for breakfast. He left Della still sleeping. He was totally surprised when he arrived at the Center. Ferguson took him into the Theater and there were at least 100 old friends, colleagues and professional archaeologists, anthropologists and geoarchaeologists that he had never met, having only read their papers on the Paleo period. He was glad to see Mike, Bill and Harry seated on the platform with him and the Colonel. The Colonel welcomed everyone and gave a brief history of the Teleportation Project. He told how Rob was selected and why Mike, Bill and Harry got involved to help him think about the possible challenges he would face.

Dr. Roby will summarize his experiences then answer specific questions.

I want to tell everyone how honored I am that I was selected to represent my colleagues on this journey. I want to give credit to Mike, Bill and Harry for their input to make my translocation successful. I have done my best to observe everything I encountered and I will publish a complete report as soon as I get some quiet time. Primarily I think the most significant thing I discovered was that the Clovis people were not Mongoloid but Caucasoid verifying the Iberian entry during this time period. Unfortunately, in my brief encounter with them I was not able to get any indication of what eventually happened to them. I understand all of you saw my Press Conference so I won't repeat that presentation but I will answer, or at least try to answer, any questions you may have.

Questions:

You mentioned a knapper at Alabates. Do you think he was the only one to do that?

He is the only one I encountered over the year's time, but while he was apparently making a living producing blades I'm sure others came to gather material and make their own artifacts.

How did the groups differ from each other?

Very little, the numbers in each were close and the male to female ratio was similar. The only exception was at the larger encampment at what we now known as the Blackwater Draw Site.

You said you were pretty sure the exchange of genes was through the movement of the males. Why did you come to that conclusion?

It really isn't a conclusion. In my observations I saw a greater need to have the right number of skilled hunters in a group so I felt the result was that the males tended to be transitional.

You mentioned cremating a child, do you think this was the preferred practice?

I think it would depend on where they were when and individual died. In that case it was expedient and appropriate but they might have buried him in a secluded rock shelter if they had been close to one like the Horn Shelter on the Brazos River north of Waco, Texas.

In your mammoth hunt and kill you said the animal had been wounded. Do you have any idea of the circumstances before you got involved?

No, unfortunately only the Village Idiot would have tried to go after a mammoth by himself. It would have been most difficult for an individual to get close enough to take a shot if the female was still connected to the herd. So I'm still not sure how it was wounded.

Was it good to eat?

Yes, it, especially the trunk, it was very good.

What is the next "step" in your opinion?

If you are referring to what period of time would I want to go back to in order to determine what happened to this particular cultural and physical group, I would want to go to a late Folsom occupation. I think they would have been encountering numerous changes, challenges and different populations. I wish the next traveler the best of luck. I hope to be around to learn the results of their venture.

Does that mean you don't want to be translocated again?

It's not that I wouldn't want to go back but I don't believe I would have the time, stamina or the fortitude to do it again. I will leave that to another, younger adventurer.

Did you see differences in the atlatl, darts, foreshafts and/or points?

Minor individual differences but as a general rule we have interpreted their tool kit pretty well. I was impressed with how well they prepared, kept and apparently how long they used their weapons. The atlatls were well worn and with a human patina on those used by the older men.

When are you going to go back and try to find the artifacts you left?

Well that's the best question I've heard since I've returned. I've got a few things to take care of at home. I have my final report to write and as I understand it individual interviews with different media outlets so just as soon as possible.

Do you think you can find some of the campsites you stayed in?

I'm hoping so. It all depends on how much things have changed over the past 13,000 years…and 12 months…laughter.

I think we've run out of time for this session but I will continue to answer your questions and explore your thoughts on my observations on my website. Let's continue the discussion. Thanks again for your support of this endeavor and my pilgrimage.

Dr. Roby has another appointment but you can continue this conversation through his website. Thank you for your interest and participation.

As they exit –What other meeting do I have?

With the plane that is taking you and Della back to Colorado.

Thank God!

We will be back in touch soon but you need and deserve some rest and quite time. The General is back in D.C. but says his door is always open.

Rob - Thanks … to everyone … for everything.

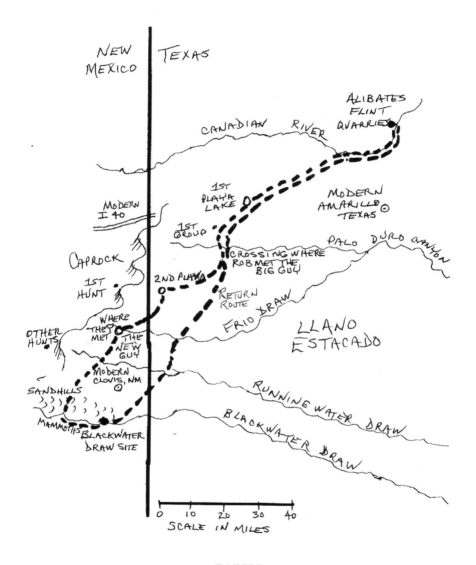

NEW MEXICO

TEXAS

ALIBATES FLINT QUARRIES

CANADIAN RIVER

1ST PLAYA LAKE

MODERN AMARILLO TEXAS

MODERN I 40

1ST GROUP

PALO DURO CANYON

CAPROCK

CROSSING WHERE ROB MET THE BIG GUY

2ND PLAYA

RETURN ROUTE

1ST HUNT

FRIO DRAW

LLANO ESTACADO

WHERE THEY MET

OTHER HUNTS

THE NEW GUY

MODERN CLOVIS, NM

RUNNING WATER DRAW

SANDHILLS

BLACKWATER DRAW

MAMMOTHS BLACKWATER DRAW SITE

BLACKWATER DRAW

0   10   20   30   40
SCALE IN MILES

**PART I**
**MAP**

# Part I

# The Players

**Dr. Robert "Rob" Roby** – 70 years old, white beard, in good shape and grew up in Colorado hunting and fishing. He attended the University of Arizona for a BA in anthropology and an MA in archaeology. Got his PhD at the University of Colorado and helped in the early stages of the development of the Institute for North American Paleo-American Research and taught there until his retirement. He has visited every known Paleo-American site and excavated several high mountain sites as well as other well established sites on the Great Plains. He has written extensively on the peopling of North America and arrival of humans from Iberia and not just Siberia based on big blade technology that was used by the Clovis people. He has lectured throughout North America and in Great Brittan, China, Russia and Japan on this new immigration premise and has stated on numerous occasions that he would like to be the first to be translocated back in time to observe the first Americans and return to the present with all the information that is not available in an archaeological context. Husband of Della and father of Nita.

**Della Roby** – trim – early 60's – beautiful with gray/white hair – wife of Rob for 40 years. Retired high school teacher – supportive and patient. Mother of Nita.

**Bruce Ferguson** – late 20's, graduate of the Air Force Academy – served his internship in social adaptations from military life to the outside world at Walter Reed Hospital and was hired to continue his work at NASA.

**Colonel Mathis (retired)** – In charge of the overall operations related to the teleportation project that involve NASA, very informed about all aspects of the protocols and internal management of the various agencies, also a major participant in the original space program and brought back as a consultant.

**General Woodward** – an earned "General" – great personal relations and management skills the latter earning him his appointment to NASA during the de-escalation of the space program.

**Dr. Harry Ross** – Paleoecologist – a colleague who has produced major papers regarding Paleo period and its environs.

**Dr. Mike Anderson** – Geoarchaeologic – a friend first and colleague second of more than 40 years.

**Dr. Bill Leftwich** – Paleoanthropologist with exceptional standing the field and knows of Rob's work.

**Dr. David Baker** – Resident physician responsible for the approval of the condition of the chosen candidate.

**Dr. Robert Ellis** – Physicist and Project Director brought in from outside to head the teleportation activities by the donor supporting the endeavor.

**The Paleo Man** – First encounter, the flint knapper at the Alibates Quarry site

**The Big Guy** – Leader of the first group Rob stayed with.

**The New Guy** – Leader of the band that joined The Big Guy's group.

**The Village Idiot** – Hit Rob in the head with a club.

**The Leader** – Leader of the third group that Rob encountered, stayed with and observed.

**The Medicine Man** – Leader of perhaps several bands who lived in a semi-permanent encampment at the Black Water Draw site.

**The Young Woman** – "Given" to him by The Medicine Man with whom he shared the rest of his journey.

**The Paleo Man** – Second encounter, the knapper who was living at the Alibates flint quarry and almost killed Rob.

**Dr. Thomas Wiley** – Psychiatrist at NASA who Rob met with when he returned from the translocation.

# Part II

# Chapter 8
# Challenges

It had been a hell of a year…Rob had isolated himself in the Hogan for almost three months writing down every detail of his journey back in time. It truly was a different, if not surreal, new journey recalling the experiences that were even hard for him to believe he had experienced. It was though he had only dreamed it but moments came back that were indelible, revealing a new sense of awareness as he could see the events from a different perspective now.

But, then the chaos ensued – interviews, appearances, lectures, collegial meetings all resulting in notoriety and recognition he never sought or desired. He understood that everyone wanted to know everything about what he encountered and just as he had done upon his return often getting caught up in the recollections enjoying answering the more intelligent questions however it was very draining physically and mentally. As he came back to the Hogan after each time consuming trip his exhaustion became accumulative but more importantly he was noticing that in his absence something was also impacting Della. He would ask but she would say she was fine.

NASA did keep all their promises and he got the dental work done and new meds for his prostate and arthritis and he and Della alternated between the Broadmoor and the Hogan. Then just before Thanksgiving she said she didn't know how much longer she could make it without doing something about her back. He knew she had been suffering for the better part of their marriage with impaired mobility but she seldom complained so he knew they had to do something soon.

He contacted their family doctor and he referred them to a specialist in Denver. Rob got on-line and checked his credentials and references finding him to be one of the best in the U.S. He called and fortunately, possibly because he knew their family doctor, he worked them in for a consultation. It was not good…her L2 and 3 had collapsed and was restricting the blood supply and had already done some nerve damage. A brace, in his opinion would no longer be effective and he recommended surgery even though that was usually his last alternative. The doctor said the longer they waited the less likelihood of a positive outcome so they scheduled the "procedure" which would reinforce the vertebrae with the insertion of a plastic device to be done just before Christmas held in place with stainless screws and rehab she should be as "good as new" in a few months.

Rob and Della went to Denver the day before the scheduled surgery and stayed in a nice hotel near the hospital. He could tell she was getting much worse and helped her get into and out of the bed. They had to be there at 5:30 AM so it was a very long but short night with little rest and, although they were terpidatious, they were hopeful this would make a major difference in their lives.

They saw the doctor only briefly as he introduced them to the head nurse and the anesthesiologist. The latter was a brash know it all who talked incessantly about everything except the procedure. He said he had looked at her chart and "everything would be fine." They told the nurse about her sensitivity to drugs of any kind and that she had experienced some severe reaction to anesthesia in the past and the nurse said that it was all recorded and that everyone involved were aware of the circumstances. Rob could tell Della was anxious and maybe had some misgivings so he tried to reassure her that they had all the protocols in place to take care of her. By that time they had given her a shot and she was feeling out of it so he kissed her as they rolled her into the prep room.

It was obviously an assembly line "operation" as all of the curtain draped cubby holes contained the doctor's patients being readied for their procedures.

Rob went out to the spacious waiting room that looked out at the snow-capped peaks to the west. He tried to read an article in one of the magazines that were scattered around on the end tables but couldn't bring his thoughts

94

around to anything other than Della. Their lives together had been a good cooperative relationship with most of their more serious disagreements occurring over their daughter, Nita. He thought Della was too strict and she thought he was too lenient but Nita had certainly turned out well having completed her Ph.D. with all kinds of recognition for her work. Rob was looking forward to calling her to tell her that her mother had come through the operation and was going to be OK.

Rob became concerned when nurse after nurse came out to tell the families of the other patients that their loved ones had come through their procedures in good shape. He finally caught one then another to ask about Della, both said they would check and get back to him. Still no word, he couldn't, wouldn't, let himself think of life without her but became increasingly more worried. He went to the "No Admittance" door and rang the bell, a nurse came out and he demanded to know how his wife was doing. The nurse said she would be right back. She did return and said Della was in recovery and he could see her in a little bit. He was able to decompress somewhat and began to write some notes in his Day-Timer for the book he was finishing about his adventure, but as more time went by and he was the last one in the waiting room he became desperate to know what was taking so long and rang the bell again. When a nurse came out he demanded to see the doctor or the nurse in charge but she informed him that she had seen Della and that they were having trouble keeping her awake so she would breath – Rob said aloud, "That damn anesthesiologist" and pushed his way through the door as the nurse said, "I will have to get approval!" Rob said, "I give you the approval!"

As he got back to the recovery area there were several individuals around the bed and a nurse was shouting at Della to "Wake Up!" She was unresponsive and limp and panic was apparent in all that were there as they rolled in the emergency equipment. Rob tried to push his way through but they kept him back saying that he would just be in the way.

They used the paddles on her chest but there was no response and an attendant called the time of death. Rob was dumbstruck with disbelief, anger, rage and was shouting at everyone wanting to know where the SOB anesthesiologist was, if he had been there he was no longer in sight. The doctor came out obviously from another operation with blood on his protective coverings and conferred with the attendant. He told Rob that she had come through the procedure in good shape but even though the anesthesiologist had "followed protocol" and given her the least amount possible that it was too much for her heart and body and that he was, "terribly sorry." "Terribly sorry!" Rob could not mount a response – it was too much and he fell to his knees, they were all around him helping him back up but he shook them off and went over to Della and broke down.

Rob didn't know how long he had been there but several people, he guessed administrators, lawyers, and the doctor who had changed into his street clothes came to comfort him and probably to make sure he was not going to sue them. He would like to have taken the anesthesiologist out behind the barn, but he wasn't going to sue anyone. He never had sued anyone and detested the charlatans who were increasing insurance rates for everyone by getting un-Godly amounts for questionable reasons and creating hardships for families who could no longer afford any kind of medical security for the future. He did have to sign the release to take her away, but he didn't even know to where. It was so final, so devastating and so unbelievable.

As it turned out her body was taken to the coroner's holding facility where all the thugs and perverts were being held but also with other corpses of other family members and he had to remind himself that they were grieving as well. He had to "claim her remains" and make preparations "for her disposition" like it wasn't a person any longer, just an object to be buried or cremated. He did know she had talked about being cremated and wanted her ashes spread on the west side of Pikes Peak where you can look out at the beginnings of the Sangre de Cristo's where they had picnicked on many spring afternoons.

Rob's most onerous and challenging responsibility lay ahead…the hardest thing he had ever faced was to call Nita and tell her of her mother's passing. Even though she and Della seldom saw anything in the same way and agreed on very few priorities they loved each other deeply. After the initial shock Nita stood strong and began to help Rob make the necessary immediate arrangements and for her flight back home.

The ceremonies, condolences and tributes were all a blur and he and Nita agreed that they would spread her ashes in the spring and wait to go through her personal things until she got back to the States. He spent a long time pondering all the causes and resulting impact of the events that had occurred. What if that, or maybe this, he could have, should have done differently that might have changed the various situations and outcome. But Nita in all her wisdom and compassion convinced him that he was never to blame in anyway and that his trust was justified and after her investigations into all of the circumstances that it was no one's fault that her mother could not have survived because of her genetic heritage. She was so sensible, so logical and so scientific that it did help him in alleviating at least some of his guilt.

If it had not been for his contractual requirement to finish the book by the deadline he most assuredly would have spiraled downward into the abyss of depression and reclusiveness. But he did complete it by the fall and did begin to notice the cat in his lap and enjoy the second cup of morning coffee again. He was looking forward to Nita returning more than he could ever remember as he had so many details to tell her about her mother that he had never shared before. He was also finding a need to show her a lot of things that would be important after his demise.

NASA had been asking him for his recommendation for a person to go on the next "mission" back, as he had suggested, to the late Folsom Period. He had been informed that they had brought in various experts including his colleagues that had been his advisors but the list thus far was full of academicians and not the "doers" that had the skills and experiences necessary to survive the arduous journey. None of the prospects were hunters or gathers in the real world...only on paper.

There was one young man Rob was aware of who was a damn good archaeologist and an active outdoorsman. His primary interest was pottery but he was very astute in lithics and knew the Paleo well enough to have co-authored a paper on sequencing and patterning of campsites from Folsom and Midland through the Plainview Period on the Great Plains. He was a good hunter, maybe too good, maybe not allowing others to take the first shot, he was gregarious, maybe a little too much so, not letting others take the lead, he was young, maybe a little too young with not quite enough experience to see the big picture and to evaluate, too quickly, challenging situations. However, Rob felt he would be far superior to those on the list and that he would ask NASA to fly him in to meet with him. At least they would know he was considering someone else and they would certainly listen to any proposals Rob would have.

Doug Riggs certainly fit the prescribed appearance, stocky, reddish beard, Nordic features and enthusiastic about everything. Rob met him at the airport and took him out to the Hogan. It was good to encounter another colleague and the conversation was most enjoyable. They shared hunting experiences and Rob was able to tell him about some of the nuances of taking pre-historic game animals that few others would understand. As they got to the discussion of Doug being the next one to be translocated back to the Folsom Period he was obviously honored if not overwhelmed that Rob was contemplating recommending him to fulfill that role. He was full of questions and pursued numerous possibilities and scenarios, but, bottom line, after much discussion he said he could not, with two small children and the possibility of not seeing them into adulthood and a wife who would not be at all understanding of the opportunity to risk his life for such an insane venture and would not be able to accept the offer. After innumerable apologies and thank-you's and a lunch of roast beef sandwiches, chips, tea and store-bought cherry pie Rob took him back to the airport for a late afternoon return flight back to Idaho.

Rob knew of no one else who could have come close to successfully completing the endeavor...except HIM! He was feeling fine physically and this would by necessity force his thoughts away from the grief but he doubted Nita would be as agreeable this time since she is now very much aware of all of the risks involved but she also knows better than anyone of his passion for knowledge and answers to the questions that have yet to be discovered.

Rob knew he would need her approval to commit to the next journey and was nervous as he began the skyping process. He told her of his disappointment in the list his colleagues had proposed and that he had found the ideal candidate but that he had regretfully declined and before he started to defend his new proposal she said, "So you need to be the one to go back?" She was surprisingly understanding, although greatly apprehensive and a little suspicious that he was the only one to achieve the next objective but she conferred her support, "with some reluctance and with the promise that you will get back safely because I will need my Dad from now on". Rob promised.

Rob decided to go to Houston as soon as it could be arranged and talk to the group about his decision that he should be the one to make the next teleportation. He didn't know what their reaction would be and at this point if they didn't agree he could easily become a recluse in the Hogan and life would be much simpler with the cat and his coffee...and memories. It had been hard "adjusting", as they say, to life without Della. His biggest deficit was his ability to figure out all of the financial ins and outs because Della had always taken care of those duties. They had grown accustomed to each other's quirks and differences, the disagreements were occasionally harsh but readily subsided and life progressed through time. He had been a faithful and hopefully a good husband as well as a loving and supportive father and at least an adequate provider and he did love both of them greatly. Maybe as expected, he would break down at something totally unexpected – a smell, a favorite cup or piece of jewelry or a coat he had bought for her that she often said, "My husband got this for me." It was particularly difficult in dealing with the routine nature of all that goes on after one loses a spouse, what is expected and how he was responding, being judged on how well he was handling "it". But he endured all of the prescribed comments and packaged condolences and he was starting to let, at least some of it, slip away and get inspired about the possible return to the past. It just might be the best thing for him now not to mention the chance to find out what happened to "his" Clovis people.

Rob called General Woodward's office number and a younger sounding lady, at least younger than the General's administrative assistant that he knew, answered, "Dr. Higgins' office how may I help you?"

Rob, a little taken aback, "I was trying to reach General Woodward"

"I'm sorry, General Woodward has retired and Dr. Higgins is the new CEO, may I say who is calling?"

"Rob Roby"

"Yes sir, please hold"

"Dr. Roby, I was hoping you would call, I'm Pat Higgins and have taken Gen. Woodward's place"

"Please, just call me Rob"

"You bet, we didn't want to disturb you or press you about your recommendation for a person to step into the next phase but let me say first, in behalf of the team here, how sorry we were to hear of your wife's passing."

"Thank you, I'm calling to ask if now is a good time for me to come back and meet you and with the group. I think I have found an answer and someone to fill your request."

"Fantastic, this is great news, since I know your advice has always been to have the person return to the Folsom Period in the late spring and we are coming up on that"

"Yes, I know"

"Let me turn you back over to my secretary and she will make all the arrangements and I will get everyone together as soon as we know your schedule, it is a real honor to speak with you and I look forward to meeting you in person, please let me know if you need anything or I can be of service in any way"

"Thanks, I'm looking forward to meeting you too"

The secretary was very considerate and competent and Rob found out that they no longer had access to the private jet and that he would be taking a commercial flight to Houston.

As he was getting ready, something was obviously worrying him, nothing specific that he could identify, just a nagging sensation that something wasn't quite right. He KNEW that Della would have NEVER agreed to a return journey and that complicated his decision. Was he trying to justify or at least explain his current thinking? Maybe guilt? Maybe Dr. Wiley could help him sort out the feelings he was experiencing...again.

Before his departure Rob called Colonel Mathis who seemed genuinely glad to hear from him and that he was on his way back down to meet with the crew. Rob asked him for a favor, to meet with Dr. Wiley first before all the other activities got in the way. The Colonel readily agreed and said he would make sure that would happen and said, "We are really looking forward to seeing you!"

Rob was met at the gate by a young man in street clothes introducing himself as Deshaun Taylor administrative aid to Dr. Higgins. When asked about General Woodward, he said that he had retired back to D.C. and that Dr. Ferguson was now teaching at the University of Nebraska and that while NASA was still part of governmental operations it was being managed by the private sector. That Dr. Patrick Higgins, a physicist had come there from Stanford University where he had been runner-up for the Nobel Prize for his work with the Supercollider when it was being planned and developed in Texas before the funding got in competition with the NASA budget.

Deshaun had been a student of Dr. Higgins but had proven himself by becoming a successful scientist and researcher in his own right being part of the team who developed the mini solar cells using Nano-technology. Rob was impressed with both of their backgrounds but, once again, they were academicians with few encounters outside their research niches. Maybe he was getting jaded in his old(er) age and maybe that was becoming a factor, or perhaps **the** factor, in evaluating colleagues in this new and rapidly changing society...and maybe, he mused, he wasn't ready for this world.

Rob was escorted into Higgins' office by his secretary, Clarisse, a trim young woman with Texas beauty pageant winning poise. The General's office had been completely refurbished, very contemporary, IKEA like, very orderly almost OCD neat. Higgins was surprisingly personable, articulate, in his mid-fifties, tall, in good shape and looked a lot like a Wall Street banker but had grown up on a farm and ranching operation in Kansas and quickly earned a little more respect from Rob.

Higgins made it clear that he only wanted to welcome him at this point and convey his willingness to be of assistance in any way possible to make him comfortable and that he would be accessible for any need he might have at any time while he was here but wanted to get him over to Dr. Wiley as soon as possible as Rob had requested and he would be available at his convenience after the meeting with Dr. Wiley.

Rob thanked him and said he would see him shortly.

Deshaun took him to Dr. Wiley's office and said he would wait on him and take him to Dr. Higgins' office when he was ready.

Dr. Wiley greeted Rob warmly and offered him coffee, which Rob gladly accepted.

Rob mentioned the obvious changes within the system and Wiley responded that it was certainly different but not all bad, he just didn't know about his future there as the new regime was evaluating everyone and some staff had retired, been replaced or the positions eliminated.

Rob said, "I will certainly put in a good word for you!"

Wiley was genuinely appreciative and glad to see Rob, even "anxious" as he expressed it, since he had not seen him since his return and was worried about him, especially since he had lost Della.

Wiley – I was truly sorry to hear about your wife and know that is weighing on you heavily, tell me how can I help you today? They said you needed to see me first...again.

Yeah Doc, you will be the first to know, my recommendation for the next person to go back is ME! I can't come up with anyone who can fully understand, comprehend or accept all the challenges inherent in the journey. I no longer have my major responsibility, that being to Della, and Nita and while she has not given me her blessing has concurred that it may be good timing and catharsis – **as long as I come back**!

Wow, I didn't see that one coming! Obviously, you have given this a lot of thought and your mind is focused on the contributions you can make, but...do you think this is this just an effort to escape all the realities you have encountered?

Well, I'm not sure Doc, I do know I'm uneasy about it because I know Della would have never approved and maybe I'm feeling a little guilty, like maybe I'm being unfaithful in some way.

And why is that?

Well, that's what I don't know. I was hoping you would have some insight.

Is your daughter in agreement with your decision?

Yes, but concerned, naturally.

It is not uncommon to keep the feelings of the deceased alive but your only responsibility at this point is to your daughter and yourself. You need to keep your wife in your thoughts but not let that control your decisions or emotions. I'm not going to say, "Move on" because everyone has a different response and time table to a life changing event, especially the loss of a loved one. However, why not wait a year, think about it some more, you might even find someone else to make the next journey that would meet your expectations.

That's a good argument Doc, but if I'm going I need to do it while I'm still able, I am in good shape now but my knees and shoulders will give out sooner or later.

You need to think about the possibility, if not the probability, that it could be sooner than later and that might hamper your ability to get back to where you need to be when the time comes. I have no doubt that we can fix you up after you get back but have you considered the multiple challenges involved with the...well, all the unknowns?

I know Doc, but I really want to do this. I want to see firsthand what these people are experiencing AND relate it to the Clovis Period and no one else has that connection.

OK, here's what I will do, IF your physical shows you to be ready, then I will be willing to, based on my original evaluation and approval, say that with some additional pre-journey analysis I **think** you will be prepared to make the second teleportation.

Thanks Doc...I couldn't have asked for any more than that and I will be looking forward to our next session.

We'll both be thinking about it...Good luck!

Deshaun was on his cell phone but dutifully waiting in the car. He said he was calling Dr. Higgins' office to let them know they were on the way.

When Rob told Higgins of his proposal and why he wanted to and needed to be the one to make the next journey he seemed relieved, then concerned.

"I'm glad we finally have someone from the standpoint of timing because we never know when the budget may be cut and if we miss this threshold there may not be another one in the offering, however, aside from the administrative issues are you up to it physically and mentally?

Rob relayed some of his conversation with Dr. Wiley and told him that it looked like he was a good candidate and that he was ready to take all of the tests and that he had no other commitments and was anxious to proceed.

Higgins said he thought everyone was available and that he would prepare a schedule and would have it to him by early in the morning and that Deshaun would take him over to the guest housing so he could get some supper and rest. "By the way, dependent on a positive result would you want us to bring in the same consultants as General Woodward did previously?"

Rob said, "If you mean Mike, Harry and Bill, you bet, I need their input on this second trip as much or more than the first one."

Higgins said he would check on their availability and alert them to the possibility of having them come back. Rob asked if they would receive the same consultant's fee and Higgins said they would.

On the way over to the guest quarters Rob realized that they might put him in the same room where he and Della had stayed and that would be too much, that he couldn't face that possibility and asked Deshaun to call ahead and ask them to put him in a different part of the facility.

By the time they arrived even if they had put him in the same room, all of the welcoming amenities had been moved to a different wing and he was deeply appreciative. He just didn't want to be that close to those memories. It was still difficult because he couldn't suppress some of the recollections but he tried to concentrate on the positive ones and not the fact that he and Della had talked about his absence, never dreaming or discussing the possibility of Della's demise.

He ordered a pizza, a Dr Pepper and some of the sweet cinnamon sticks and made some notes about what he and his "consultants" should address. There were many, the time period is fraught with challenges of weather, changes in habitat, and decreasing populations of both game and people…except for those immigrating in through the ice-free corridor. All, actually each element had many facets with each needing much discussion.

He had slept well and Deshaun had a copy of the schedule for him when they met the next morning. Deshaun said Colonel Mathis sent his regrets that he wouldn't be able to see him this time that he had some commitments he had to keep. He was to see Dr. Ellis first, who as Rob learned had taken over as the Project Director, because the Colonel was being reassigned to other duties elsewhere since the private contractor had come aboard.

They met in Ellis' office which seemed even more cluttered than Rob had remembered, if that was even discernable, but he was sincere in his regrets about Della's passing. Rob congratulated him for being promoted and he abruptly replied, "Just more work and responsibility, but I am glad to see you and hear your thoughts on who you are recommending to take the next giant leap".

After telling Ellis about his decision to continue the journey since he was the most logical choice and the one they could count on to know the best way to get back and make it a successful venture. Rob also gave a condensation of his meetings with Dr. Wiley and the new CEO he felt he had made a good argument in his behalf. Ellis showed the same reticence as displayed by Wiley and expressed great concern about his mental stability for even considering yet another challenge of this magnitude, but acquiesced saying he would do everything in his power to bring him back a second time…as long as Dr. Baker approved his continued physical fitness.

Ellis walked him through the facility showing him some improvements and said that the most significant advancement was their ability to bring him back from a different location than where he is deployed as long as they have a GPS reading on exactly where the pickup site is to be. That was great news and opened up a lot more possibilities than Rob had previously considered but Ellis cautioned, "It still must be exactly a year or 2 or 3 now, with the 2-3 day boundary of time because the 'window' is still the limiting factor in the process even though there is more latitude as to when we send you". Rob acknowledged the warning.

Deshaun arrived a little before noon and took both of them to Higgins' office. Dr. Wiley and Dr. Baker were already there and it was a duplicate of Rob's first meal there with the General, salad, T-bones, baked potatoes, pintos, fresh bread and cobbler. Baker came over quickly and greeted him with, "I hear from these guys that you have a determined case of ignorance."

Rob replied, "I guess I've always had a problem with that but it seems that it has gotten me out of as much as it has gotten me into."

"Well put, I admire your resiliency as much as your tenacity, let's eat."

Dr. Baker said he would have only one opinion and that would be based on what his physical revealed, but added, "If this is your desire I hope it goes well."

Most of the conversation centered on what Rob believed he might encounter if he was selected for the next translocation. He related the possibilities to what he had experienced in his last excursion into the Pleistocene and it went well. Everyone seemed to be enthralled about the next potential visit, maybe especially Higgins, whose questions were well formulated and probing. They all seemed relaxed and lingered into the afternoon with Rob enjoying the camaraderie as well. They parted offering support and encouragement but with Dr. Baker telling Rob that wanted him to start fasting with nothing after 6 PM and to take the usual horrendous pre-exam preparations that should be in his room by the time he gets there and be in his office at 6 AM in the morning.

Rob cringed but was OK with the admonition as he had enjoyed the lunch more than anything he had been a part of since Della's passing.

Deshaun asked him if he needed to go anywhere or if he needed anything before he went back to his room. Rob said he had his laptop and that was all he required until morning as long as was at the doctor's office by 6…Deshaun said he would pick him up at 5:30 on the dot.

Rob was both introspective and contemplative the rest of the evening but still did not question his decision. It was not a restful night but he made himself do all the necessary procedures and met Deshaun at 5:30AM.

He got to the doctor's office as scheduled and went through the tedious process including an eye, hearing and stress test, a colonoscopy, endoscopy, X-rays, MRI and CAT scan with no relief or compassion. These people were very clinical and efficient and he was more than ready for lunch but Dr. Baker wanted him to see the dentist first.

Dr. Sarah Moore was the young looking, middle-age, very attractive woman who had taken care of Rob's dental needs the previous year and in awe of all that Rob was planning when they met and then what he had accomplished in the first teleportation, obviously she had read all of the reports and asked some extremely piercing questions about what he had eaten, what his and the Paleo people's dental hygiene was like and a myriad of other minutia that he had to contend with while on his journey. She also said she would like to learn more about the whole trip and the people he encountered at some point in the future. She added that as soon as he was approved for the next venture she would have to remove the implants and that it would take several weeks for the healing process before she would release him. When Rob tried to pin down the timing she became defensive saying that it would all depend on how rapidly he recovered and she wouldn't know that until she saw him sometime after the process. She did, however, say that she was excited to be part of the project and would be looking forward to replacing his new implants when he returned from the Folsom Period.

Rob finally got to the late lunch with Higgins and again it was a repeat of what they had offered in the past. A sandwich spread with a fresh fruit salad, homemade potato chips, ice tea and cheesecake for dessert. Higgins was very positive and affirmative in his approval of Rob's proposal and obviously wanted to proceed as soon as they got a "go". He had contacted Mike, Bill and Harry and each said they would do what was necessary to come as soon as they were called. He shared with Higgins Ellis' comments about fine tuning the retrieval so that it could be at a different location and greater leeway for the timing of the pickup but more importantly, for any future translocations they had identified more cyclic opportunities that would allow for greater variability in when they could send and recover new voyagers. Rob also discussed Wiley's need to sign off on his mental state and expressed his concern over how long Dr. Moore's release might take dependent on the duration of his healing. They both agreed that Wiley was always challenging the status quo and that Sarah was a strong-willed woman but neither one of them should delay the project significantly. While they were waiting on the results of the physical Higgins wanted Rob to meet with Ellis again and bring him up to speed on having to be cleared by Dr. Wiley and the possible postponement suggested by Dr. Moore and make sure he had all the details under consideration.

Rob wanted to get out of the various enclosures so he walked over to Ellis' office. It was already hot but the humidity was more oppressive than the heat and he sweated down quickly. He almost hiked on over to the guest housing but thought better of it and decided he would call Deshaun later to take him over to get a shower.

Ellis was up to his ears in paper work but welcomed him in commenting with obvious disdain about how bureaucratic the system was becoming and didn't know how much longer he could take it. Rob thanked him for all of his past and current support and encouragement and commiserated on how glad he was to retire when he did since he was spending all of his time filling out unintelligible forms. Ellis said a possible delay was no longer a problem that they had expanded their window of opportunity greatly and it would be fine. He went on to postulate a probable need for Rob's experiences for a continuing consultancy in the future which could be advantageous for him financially. Rob thanked him for the confidence expressed and for thinking of him for the potential opportunity.

Almost on cue Deshaun appeared at the door to check on him and said Dr. Higgins wanted him to know that he had some free time the rest of the day, at least until they heard from Dr. Baker which would probably not be until the next morning. Deshaun took him back to his quarters and said he would pick him up at 8 AM to go to Dr. Baker's office to confer on the results of the physical.

Rob was still hungry and ordered his now usual, crawfish etouffe and bar-beque combo and enjoyed it as much as before. He wanted to skype Nita but decide to wait until he found out the final outcome. He caught up in his journal the many events that had brought him to this point knowing that Nita would be interested in reading it someday.

Rob met with Baker the next morning after a short wait. They had speeded up the analysis and there were few surprises, arthritis in most of the joints, damaged knees and shoulders, hiatal hernia, small cluster of kidney stones and a prostrate that was still enlarged but smooth. But, taking everything into con-sideration Baker said he was in very good health for a 60 year old and damn good shape for a 70 year old male of the *Homo sapiens* species. He had cleared the next to the last hurdle with only one thing remaining, his next session with Dr. Wiley, not counting of course, the extraction of his implants.

Wiley couldn't see him until mid-afternoon but Higgins had invited him back to his office for lunch if he had finished with Baker so he walked over to the administration complex. It was much nicer in the mornings with a cool breeze from the Gulf and he wanted to make a request of Higgins so it had worked out nicely.

Higgins had received the news that Rob had passed Baker's inspection and congratulated him on negotiating the successful maze thus far. The lunch was the same fare as the day before and if Rob was guessing it was the left-over's but it was still good. Rob's request was that his three colleagues/consultants be allowed to come to the Broadmoor and his Hogan rather than Houston.

This would allow for a much more relaxed and conducive setting to plan for his next excursion. Higgins readily agreed and added that they should take all the time they needed, that his budget would cover all expenses. Rob thanked him for not only his interest but also his commitment to the project. Higgins asked his secretary to call Deshaun and have him come pick up Rob and take him to Dr. Wiley's office.

Wiley said that he didn't have anyone else scheduled for the rest of the afternoon and they would have plenty of time. They just visited for a good while, more as friends than doctor/patient and Rob truly appreciated the atmosphere, feeling he had finally found someone who really did understand what he had been through and it helped a lot to get the feedback. But, when he told Wiley that everything had been endorsed by everyone but him, his demeanor changed and he became the interrogator again, questioning Rob's reasoning, challenging his thought process and reiterating how he was tempting fate to enter into all the obstacles that he was sure to face. After a lengthy discussion with each trying to understand the other's the feelings, concerns and especially Rob's defense of his goals Wiley said he would not stand in the way of Rob's determination to make this a successful endeavor. Wiley wished him Godspeed and said he was always at the end of the line, or net, if Rob wanted to discuss **anything** that was a problem, big or small.

Deshaun, once again, as if he was clairvoyant, was walking up to the door as Rob was leaving. As they were on their way to Rob's room he asked Deshaun to get him in to see Dr. Moore as soon as possible the next morning and that he would like to fly out as soon as he could after the appointment. Deshaun said he would take care of it adding that Dr. Higgins would like to see him before his departure and would have lunch ready before he left if he had time. Rob said that would be fine but he probably wouldn't be able to eat anything after the extractions. Deshaun responded with the assurance that he would forward that bit of information. Rob skyped Nita and they had a long talk as he explained everything that had transpired during the last few days. He told her how he had been approved by all the examiners and all he had remaining was the extractions. He also told her that Mike, Bill and Harry would be coming to the Springs to consult which would be a lot better for him. She was glad that everything had gone well but remained a little terpidatious imploring him to take care of himself and to call her when he got home. He promised he would. They agreed he would pay for her to come back home around her mother's birthday at the end of March so they could spread her ashes and she said she would plan on it and let him know when she could get away.

Rob was in Moore's office at 8 AM and waited half an hour before she came in. As she passed by him on the way in she said, "It looks like you are the priority around here." An aid took him into her examining room about 15 minutes later. She revealed that Higgins had called and asked her to get Rob in and out ASAP adding that he also told her that everything had been approved for his next teleportation. She then shocked Rob by saying, "I wish I could go with you." It took him a minute to respond, "Well, that would be alright with me." He was clambering for a more appropriate retort but before he could come up with something witty she said, "Seriously, what all did you have to do to get ready for such an awesome adventure?" So he went into detail about getting his feet prepared, eating some almost tainted meat, updating his knapping abilities, getting his first artificial tan and of course getting his teeth pulled which she performed. He explained all of this while she was working on his extractions. Her response was startling, "I could handle all of that but you would have to teach me how to knap." Rob was speechless, he had no come back and his mind was racing back and forth. He had never once considered someone going with him; it was preposterous, it was going to take all of his energies just to survive himself much less having a woman, a beautiful, very modern looking woman, along. Especially one who has no concept of the challenges or conflicts that she might encounter or engender coming in contact with the Paleo population or all of the hardships and new unknowns he was going to confront in this next journey. Before he could answer she said, "But, at this point I guess it is out of the question, I'll just have to get you ready and live vicariously through your experiences." Rob was more than relieved, he was overjoyed, he did not know what he would have done if she had pursued this line of thinking with Higgins or Ellis or Wiley, they might have thought it was a good idea. When she finished she made him promise that she would be one of the first people to hear everything that had happened and she kissed him on the cheek and said be careful and that she would be thinking about him while he was gone. Her aid gave him a round of antibiotics and said they would need to see him in two weeks and to call if he had any problems.

Deshaun was waiting to take him to Higgins' office but Rob was not feeling up to much conversation and certainly no food. He asked Deshaun if he would call Higgins and graciously decline the invitation and go by and pick up his baggage and head for the airport with the possibility of catching an earlier flight. Deshaun called and Higgins was most understanding and said he would see him in a couple of weeks. Rob asked to speak to Higgins and asked him to let his advisors/consultants know he would call them in a few days to set up their trips to the Springs. Higgins said he would do it immediately.

Apparently Higgins' secretary had already called the airlines and had gotten him on the flight back with a first class seat, probably the only way they could make a change that quickly. He was most appreciative and the stewardess made him a smoothie which he enjoyed greatly.

He had left the SUV at the airport and drove to the Broadmoor as he was still feeling a little out of it and decided to stay there for a few days so he didn't have to fix his own meals or do anything but try to heal as quickly as possible. It was nice, even lavish, but it wasn't home and he was thinking he might offer to give it back if they would build him a guest house next to the Hogan. That would save them a lot of money in the exchange and it would serve his needs much better in the future.

He was able to get in touch with Mike, Bill and Harry the next day and they all agreed to come in the following week. Each berated him for even thinking he should be the one to go back but would take that up with him when they got there. He felt he really needed to get back to the Hogan so left the Broadmoor early the next morning.

There was a cloud bank to the south and the sunrise spread a soft reddish-pink glow over the mountains as he got to his and Della's road. The pet sitter had taken good care of Cat and she only wanted to be brushed. She settled in on his lap and he enjoyed a second cup of coffee which seemed especially good, maybe because he was home, in his favorite recliner and where he wanted to stay. The memories here were distinctly different from NASA or the Broadmoor, the Hogan seemed to hold lasting and permanent positive recollections of his and Della's and Nita's lives together. Maybe it really is the little things and times are the best in the long run. It was, as one of his friends said, "… one of the most comfortable places he had ever been."

He readied himself to meet with his colleagues, making notes on things he wanted and needed to discuss about the next entrada. Where would he have the best chance to meet up with the Folsom people, what can he expect in the environment, what would the weather be like, where and what resources he would require to survive a year…or more. And timing, everything revolved around trying to interpret what he would encounter during a certain time period. Each of these questions had a host of ramifications and he wanted their input to supplement his thinking just as they had done before. He knew they were going to be even tougher on him this time since they thought he was out of his mind for attempting his first lunacy. This trip was probably going to be much more unpredictable and dangerous. Rob knew from his experience and research that the Carbon 14 dating showed that the greatest concentration for the Folsom Period fell between 11,500 and 10,900 years before the present and given the low density of long term sites, an indication that they were highly mobile and dispersed with small groups of people apparently heavily dependent on giant bison for subsistence, it was apparent that even locating them would be chancy. Taking down one of these large animals would, as in the case of the Clovis Period, require communal hunting practices and thus their family units would tend to be characterized by either a disproportionate number of males or necessitate joining with members of other "tribes" to hunt specific areas at a predetermined time and place. There is evidence that they were utilizing the inter-montane edges between the mountains and the plains during the late summer or early fall when they could take advantage of small bands of cows, calves and yearlings before the smaller groups began herding together for the winter.

# Chapter 9

# Consultations

**M**ike was the first to arrive and Rob was glad as he had known Della well and they got to reminisce about some of the good times they had shared in the early days of building their careers. Mike was more understanding of Rob's desire to return than anyone thus far and wanted to be supportive by helping him think through all of the options and come up with the best scenario for his successful return. He made it clear that he was majorly concerned for his safety and even his survival, more so this time around given all the circumstances surrounding the Folsom Period. But they agreed to wait on the others before getting bogged down with all of the uncertainties at this point and just visit.

Rob grilled some steaks and baked potatoes for supper and made waffles, bacon and eggs for breakfast.

They met Harry at 10:30 AM at the airport and waited until 11:30 for Bill to arrive who's first words of wisdom were, "What's all this craziness about? They told me some idiot was trying to go back to the Folsom Period!" That spurred some interest from travelers coming in and trying to board their flights and some recognized Rob and wanted to take pictures and get autographs. Fortunately that attention had died down considerably for which he was extremely grateful.

Rob took them to the Broadmoor for lunch, which was, as usual, a big spread and very good. He said they could stay there but thought they would be able to deliberate much better at the Hogan and all agreed. Mike told the other two that they really needed to see what Rob and Della had built as well as the setting…they both said they were anxious to finally get the chance to visit there.

Rob only fixed sandwiches for supper and they all consented to just visit but the conversation turned to Rob's first relocation and the use of the landscape by the Clovis people and what ecological relationships might continue to be present in the Folsom Period. They stayed up later than Rob had expected for the first night but it was a good introduction for the next day.

Rob fixed homemade biscuits, eggs, ham and lots of coffee for breakfast he also had some Colorado honey and last year's peach preserves Della had put up. He began the conversation with a totally radical proposal…that he somehow find his way to the Lindenmeier site in extreme northern Colorado. Naturally, each of them were well acquainted with the largest Folsom campsite ever found and the extensive excavations through the years that have produced thousands of artifacts and bone fragments giving archaeologists the best picture of their cultural identity and that's when the discussions got serious.

Mike – Why not just go back to Blackwater Draw, we know there is also a heavy concentration of Folsom represented there?

Bill – Yeah, you would know the territory and best routes and wouldn't be guessing your way and possibly wasting valuable time trying to find these people.

Rob – That's all true but the dates seem more scattered at Blackwater than at Lindenmeier which are pretty solid at a median of 11,500 BP.

Harry – So that is when you want to go back, to that specific date?

Rob – Well I'm open to debate but I think I would catch someone there at that time.

Harry – The Younger Dryas occurred from maximums of 12,900 BP to 11,700 BP dependent on the location in altitude and/or latitude so you would be closer to the end of the cold dry climatological change but in all probability not as comfortable as you found in Clovis times, in fact you might freeze you ass off during the winter.

Mike – And you will really have to work to find adequate water sources. If it isn't here today it's not going to be there then and you would also be right in the end of the mass extinctions which means you certainly wouldn't find as much game as you did earlier.

Bill – There is the consideration that all of us want to know what was happening with the population at that point and since Lindenmeier is certainly active at then it would make sense to shoot for that date.

Mike – I'm not so sure…you may be right on the edge of their existence and if these people are under severe environmental stress and/or they are being overrun by other groups who don't like the way they look or smell or talk even with a marginal plus or minus on the C14 dates you might be better off to go a little earlier.

Rob – Good point.

Harry – I bet it would be even colder.

Rob – So what do you suggest?

Harry – Let me think about it.

Mike – So where do you want to be deposited?

Rob – That is the biggest question I have for you guys. Ellis tells me they can pick me up at a different location this time as long as they have the exact coordinates.

Mike – Well that is good news as long as you make it to where ever and know without question that is the same place you identify with the GPS.

Rob – Yeah, I know, I was thinking, since we know that they were utilizing the draws along the Front Range and we know they were scattered, few in numbers and apparently very mobile, that I would start out back at Alibates.

Harry – And walk all the way to northern Colorado and survive?

Mike – I agree, how far is that?

Rob – I figure 615 miles if I follow the Canadian into NM to be sure of having permanent water, then up through the Folsom Type Site to the Cimarron taking advantage of the tinajas, then hitting any one of the creeks running into the Arkansas and following the opposing creeks north crossing over into the Platt drainages to Lindenmeier.

Bill – That's even further than from Alibates to Gault that we discussed the last time.

Rob – But I wouldn't have the return trip.

Harry – But I don't think you could make it in a year taking everything into consideration.

Rob – You mean my age?

Harry – Hell no, I think you probably can make it physically IF you can find the resources but it would certainly be difficult for any human under the conditions we've already discussed.

Mike – Why not just land near Lindenmeier and get picked up there?

Rob – What if I am off a plus or minus a couple of hundred years? The chance of meeting up with some Folsom person is much greater the greater distance traveled. And I can take advantage of my knowledge of Alibates and the shelter and at least some of the resources I know about so I can get a good start.

Bill – On the other hand you might be accepted into the camp at Lindenmeier immediately, but even if you had to wait a few months before they returned you would still have the same resources they had for several hundred years at that site.

Rob – But what about a lithic quarry, I am not familiar with a good source of knappable material in the immediate area and that was critical in my last journey.

Mike – There are the Knife River quarries in North Dakota but that's a pretty good hike as well. I think Rob's plan has some merit. He knows the plains, and mountains for that matter, here in Colorado and can get NASA to fly him over the proposed route and pick out good potential rest stops that would provide food and water, hopefully, and even averaging a few of miles a day he could make it. By the way I want to go with you on that flight this time.

Bill – But his chances of an accident or hostile encounter with a mean tempered mammal increases exponentially the more miles traveled.

Harry – That was my point. It ain't gonna' be easy no matter what course you take and the less obstacles you put in the way the better chance you have of making it back alive.

Rob – It's time for lunch so let's take a break and I am going to fix us some turkey sandwiches from the one I got in the fall. I smoked it and it has been real good so far.

Mike – You mean you haven't started to eat some more tainted meat?

Rob – Not yet and that isn't the last of that story.

After lunch, which they all seemed to enjoy Rob brought out some Midland-like Points he had made from the Alibates he had from the exploratory trip he made before his last expedition.

Rob – I'm not that good with the fluting but from what I can find in the literature about 10% of the points in Folsom sites are unfluted Midland-like, so I think, considering my old age that I can get by with just Midland-Plainview points in my tool kit.

116

Harry – Let me defend myself, I never implied anything about your old age in fact that will probably really work to your advantage this time around as well because they will be looking for all the help they can get.

Mike – The question is…what will the new immigrants from Beringia think about a white bearded old man?

Bill – If, in fact he encounters them. We still don't know if the Folsom people just died out, starved out, were wiped out by Nano diamonds, got over-run by other *Homo sapiens* sub-species or were assimilated, at least maybe Rob can find out.

Harry – As long as he doesn't find out first hand and prevent him from getting back here to let us know.

Rob – Now it is getting too depressing so I'm going to fix some Pronghorn that's been in the freezer and needs to be eaten.

Mike – Roadkill?

Rob – Not this time, do you guys want an old fashion Coors while you wait? All responded positively, with enthusiasm.

Rob fried up the Pronghorn back strap he had been saving for a special occasion and fixed home fried potatoes, home canned green beans from Della's garden, left over biscuits and lots of cream gravy. They apparently enjoyed the meal because they left nothing in the bowls or on their plates. The conversation around the dinner table continued to explore the if's, and's and but's, but all were now behind him trying to help him make the best decisions possible before he got into the reality of actually trying to traverse 600 miles on foot in a very uncompromising environment.

The next morning over pancakes, eggs and sausage and lots of coffee they agreed that they could probably communicate by email in the future and the advisors/consultants should get back to this world and their responsibilities.

Rob called Higgins' secretary to make the arrangements and she said that they would probably have to get first class seats to accomplish the request so quickly and Rob encouraged that approach hoping they would get a positive experience as an end note.

By the time the guys got their gear together she called back and said, "Mission accomplished, they all leave around noon and I am emailing their boarding tickets and yes they are all first class". Rob thanked her profusely and said he would be back in touch in a couple of weeks to make his appointment with Dr. Moore.

They got to the airport in good shape and Rob was able to let them all out at the same gate. He reiterated how much he enjoyed having them come and especially how important it was to have their counsel, debate and direction in setting his mental compass for his next venture. They all wished him luck and Mike reminded him that he wanted to be on board when he flew the route from Alibates to Lindenmeier. Rob said he would let him know.

Rob had gained weight and needed to get in shape to be ready for the next journey. He began to work out and recondition his feet but he didn't go looking for any road kills. He also practiced making Midland-Plainview points and casting darts with the lighter points to make sure he was proficient with the smaller technological product.

He was almost a week late in making the appointment with Dr. Moore and Higgins' secretary must have gotten the OK to continue to get first class seats for him. Deshaun picked him up and as Rob had requested went to Higgins' office first. He told Higgins about the consultation with his colleagues and their agreement of his proposal to go from Alibates to Lindenmeier and asked if he could get a fly over of the area before his relocation as he had done previously flying the route to the Clovis site. Higgins was very supportive and said that while he wasn't familiar with the new protocols he would begin making the arrangements. Rob added that he would like for Mike to make the tour with him and Higgins agreed.

He found out that Sarah wouldn't be available until late afternoon so he went to see Ellis.

He told Ellis about his proposed drop off at Alibates as before but his desire to be picked up at Lindenmeier a year later. Ellis said he would need the GPS coordinates as soon as possible and Rob told him about the fly over and that he would send them as soon as he could.

Higgins had invited him back to his office for lunch which was pleasant and enjoyable with Rob telling him more about the meeting with Mike, Bill and Harry and many of the considerations they discussed. Higgins was very interested and commented on how detailed their deliberations were and that he was glad to be a part of the endeavor.

Rob asked Higgins' secretary to call and see if Dr. Wiley might be available for a short visit before he saw Dr. Moore. She said that Dr. Wiley was available until 3 PM and to come on over anytime.

Wiley was glad to see Rob and wanted to know how it had gone with his colleagues and where he was with his plans. Rob shared all of the recent events including the meetings he had earlier that day. He asked specifically about how he was doing adjusting to not having Della in his life. That generated a lengthy conversation that resulted in some more closure for Rob. As usual, it was always helpful to have Wiley's rational translation of Rob's feelings.

He got to Sarah's office early but he was glad to have some reflective time to consider everything that was occurring in his life now, especially after his visit with Wiley.

The assistant took Rob into the empty examining room. When Sarah came in he said, "Hello Doc," which generated an immediate response, "Don't call me 'Doc'…just Sarah." "Yes ma'am." "And don't call me 'ma'am'". "OK, **Sarah.**"

Let me see how you are doing…looks good, you are a quick healer. So what has happened since I saw you?

Rob, recounted everything including the yet to be scheduled fly over whereupon she said she wanted to go. This woman was incomparable; she had an insatiable appetite for knowledge and adventure. Rob responded with the only thing he could come up with at the moment, "I'll have to do some checking and let you know". To which she replied, "If you have anyone telling you "no" let me know and I will take care of it." She was obviously pretty damned determined too.

She said she had worked him in and that she had another patient waiting but that she would be waiting on a call to let her know when they were going on the excursion. She gave him a quick but warm hug and left.

Rob went back to Higgins' office and waited until he had a break and told him about Sarah's desire to fly with he and Mike over the route he had picked out. Higgins said he had no objection as long as she scheduled it around her appointments but that was still trying to get everything arranged and it might be feasible. He added that she would probably have to take some of her leave and he couldn't pay for her expenses to get to Colorado Springs as it looked like they would be flying out of Peterson Air Force Base. Rob said he would forward those parameters on to her and asked if it was possible he could head back home that night. Higgins said his secretary would try to arrange it and that he would get back to him as soon as he finalized the fly over. Rob thanked him for all that he was doing to make the undertaking successful and Higgins replied, "Thank you, for all **you** are doing and risking!" His secretary was able to get Rob a first class seat on the last flight to the Springs in just a few minutes and called Deshaun to come pick up Rob.

He called Sarah and told her of Higgins' restrictions, and she said, "No problem, I'll be ready".

The next few days were consumed in looking at Google images of the proposed route and he continued to prepare himself for the flight and eventual journey. He did identify a small hill near the Lindenmeier National Landmark that looked like a good place to be picked up and decided to drive up and look at it closer. He had been to Lindenmeier on several occasions taking his students on field trips to see the site first hand but had never viewed it from this new perspective. At this point in its geological history it is very identifiable with little likelihood of much change since the Pleistocene so he took a GPS reading right on top of the hill.

On the way home he got a call on his cell phone from Higgins and everything had been arranged and that they would be able to take a helicopter out of Peterson on May 1st and that he had approved Sarah's leave of absence.

Rob called Mike and gave him the specifics and said if he was available he would call Higgins' secretary and have her schedule him into the Springs a few days early so they could go over what Rob had found to look for on the flight and, "Oh, by the way Sarah Moore the dentist from NASA will be coming along...I'll explain when I see you". Mike responded, "Most interesting, yes, I will be available and do I get a first class seat again?" Rob said, "I'll see what I, or actually, what they can do".

Nita was able to fly in a few days before her Mother's birthday. She had caught a cold and had major jet lag so slept in the first day back. Rob cooked all the meals even though she liked to cook for them when she came back home. He went over a lot of the necessary paperwork that accompanied the estate that related not only to Della but also to him in case, or actually when, something happens to him. She understood the reason for doing so but became dejected and sad and said they needed to go to the picnic spot the next day. He agreed and made their usual egg salad sandwiches, fruit salad and took her Mother's favorite cheesecake from the Broadmoor. The day was both sublime and depressing but they both agreed that was what she would have wanted them to do. Before she left they talked a lot about what they wanted to accomplish around the place when she got back home for a longer visit. They held each other for a long time and cried together before she got on the plane to leave.

# Chapter 10

## The Excursion

Mike did get first class and made it in on the 28th of April and he and Rob went over everything that might give them pause that they needed to look for on the flight. He fixed some venison, potatoes and gravy for supper and bacon, eggs and biscuits for breakfast the next morning. They picked up Sarah about 11 AM on the 29th and had lunch at the Broadmoor and brought her up to speed on the next day's excursion. Rob gave her the choice of staying at the Broadmoor or going on out to the Hogan. She wanted to see the Hogan but since neither one of them had been Rob drove them up to the top of Pikes Peak before going to the Hogan. Sarah was fascinated with the concept, how it was built and that Rob and Della had done it themselves. Rob grilled elk steaks, baked potatoes and had a side salad and wine which they enjoyed along with the conversation about the next day's adventure.

They had to be at Peterson by 8 AM sharp on the 1st of May but Rob was able to have his homemade waffles, venison sausage, scrambled eggs and coffee ready at 6 AM. They left at 7 AM and got to the Air Force Base at 8 AM. Their conveyance was a Blackhawk helicopter and they flew straight to the Amarillo Airport and refueled. The pilot then flew over the Alibates National Landmark and west up the Canadian River. Rob pointed out where he had stayed in the shelter and his first course of travel then started to take dozens of digitals from that point on. They started up the river to where I 25 crosses it south of Raton, New Mexico then went northeast skirting the west side of Capulin volcano and right over the Folsom Type Site then looked for a crossing along the Cimarron into Colorado. Sarah saw a good place on her side of the copter and pointed it out. They then followed one of the Trinchera tributaries which had the most water then down to the Purgatoire following it to the Arkansas River. The pilot then broke into the chatter between them to say he had to go back to Peterson to refuel but that they would come back to that spot to continue.

They took a short break and got some snacks and drinks at the vending machines before heading out again. The pilot set a northwestwardly course from where they had crossed the Arkansas River and this was where Rob needed a lot of close surveillance because there were limited water resources currently across that part of the landscape. With both Mike's and Sarah's help he was able to take pictures of the most plausible ones to choose from. He felt he could easily identify the most promising one by comparing his digitals with the Google maps. As they got closer to Lindenmeier he could see the hill he had visited and asked the pilot if he could set down on top of it. They made a circle around it and he was able to land right where Rob had selected to be picked up. They got out for a few minutes and Rob was able to point out the site and explain what he hoped to achieve while there. He asked the pilot to take a GPS reading so he could compare what he had gotten on his hand held one.

They got back just as the sun was setting behind the mountains with a golden and orange sunset. They went to the Broadmoor for supper and Sarah said she would stay there for the night and take the shuttle for her flight back early the next morning. As they said good bye she told Rob she had never had a better day. She hugged him and kissed him on the cheek and said that she would see him before his "lift off".

That evening Rob and Mike went over the whole trip selecting the digitals that helped them choose the best possible scenario for the most challenging areas.

Rob fixed them some oatmeal, toast and coffee before taking him to the airport. Mike said it had been a great experience and he would treasure it always. He wished Rob the best of luck and perseverance and to let him know when the "lift off" would be so he could mark his calendar for the pick-up... Rob promised he would.

Rob didn't want to be alone that evening so stayed at the Broadmoor and was very contemplative through the evening meal.

He called Ellis the next day to confirm the pilot's and his GPS readings and ask what date he thought would be favorable for "lift off". Ellis asked if he was ready physically and mentally. Rob answered affirmatively. Ellis said he believed the 15th was good. Rob said he would come in on the 10th for the final evaluations and would see him then.

Rob became a little anxious after the date was set and skyped Nita to tell her about all of the decisions that had been made over the past few days. They made plans for her to be at NASA when he returned. She reiterated how important it was for him to be careful and get back safely and he promised he would...although both of them knew that this journey was probably going to be even more challenging than the previous expedition.

Rob attended to a myriad of last minute details, including the house/pet sitter for Cat and making sure that if he didn't make it back Nita would have everything she needed at her fingertips to handle the estate including the possibility of exchanging the room at the Broadmoor for a guest house but that would be her decision, maybe even after he returns.

When he got to Houston Intercontinental and Deshaun was waiting to pick him up and take him to his room in the guest facility. He had lots of notes and greeting from the well-wishers who knew about his commitment to be on the next teleportation including General Woodward and Colonel Mathis and of course Mike, Bill and Harry. There was also a card from Sarah who wrote that she wanted to take him to dinner any evening he chose before his departure. He wasn't sure he should encourage the relationship for a plethora of reasons, not the least of which centered on the success or failure of the mission.

His first appointment the next morning was with Ellis who went over all the pre-translocation procedures with no notable differences from the last time. He would meet with Baker, Wiley, Moore and Higgins who wanted him to come to lunch at noon. Ellis confirmed the day, time, locations of deposit and return and verified the GPS coordinates. Everything was a go on the 15th and Rob began to feel anxious again, but this time it was a positive exhilaration with the expectation of getting on with the effort. He was ready!

Higgins had barbeque, potato salad, pinto beans, cornbread, tea and cobbler for their lunch. He admitted that he had selfishly not included anyone else for their visit because he wanted to mention a few things that were personal to Rob. Higgins led off with the verification that all of the commitments that had been made to he and Della would continue to be honored in behalf of Nita. That in case of his non-retrieval the Broadmoor room, the annual remuneration and the health related insurances would all be transferred to Nita as long as she is alive. Rob was greatly appreciative and relieved as that had not been discussed since Della's passing and his commitment to make the second journey.

Seeing the opening he asked Higgins if it might be possible to exchange the Broadmoor room for a guest house next to the Hogan, pointing out that it would be a big savings to their budget in the long run. Higgins said that he would do some checking and try to let him know before his departure. Rob added that it would need to be Nita's decision if he didn't make it back. Higgins concurred and said he had one more item that he needed to share, "This is not easy for me as I rarely get involved in an employee's personal affairs but I felt you should know that Dr. Moore's husband was killed in an automobile accident last year and while she has been in therapy she is still extremely vulnerable and may need more time to adjust to her loss…I probably approved her return a little prematurely". Rob replied, "I understand and acknowledge my mental fragility as well. I had already decided to not pursue any relationship at this time…even more so now since hearing of the loss of her husband, I certainly would not want her to experience any additional trauma." "Thanks, Rob, I knew you would understand, let's eat". They enjoyed each other's company long into the afternoon talking about what Rob expected to encounter on his way to Lindenmeier and Higgins showing him one of his prized possessions, an "arrowhead" he had found as a boy, that as Rob explained, was actually an Archaic dart point, approximately 4,000 years old, and, "a fine one at that."

Higgins said he was scheduled to meet with Dr. Wiley the next morning and Dr. Moore in the afternoon and his final physical with Dr. Baker would be on the 14th the day before "lift off". As Rob was leaving he thanked Higgins' secretary for her assistance with all of the arrangements she had accomplished in his behalf. She wished him the best of luck and said she would be looking forward to hearing about his newest travels.

Deshaun took him to his room and said to call him if he needed anything. Rob wished he could move everything up a notch and leave a day earlier but there were too many wheels already in motion so he would have to make the best of it.

He ordered a T-bone, baked potato and pecan pie for his supper and thought a lot about his future after…if he made it back, maybe Sarah might be a part of it but he was not ready for either one of them to get that involved at this point.

Rest was elusive but after a breakfast buffet he felt refreshed and was looking forward to seeing Wiley who welcomed him into his office with the offer of another cup of coffee. Rob told him about the reconnaissance of the route and how much the consulting with his colleagues helped and then about his unexpected association with Sarah. Wiley all but said he knew about it but when Rob asked if he was her counselor, he said he couldn't say. Wiley did agree they should probably feather their engines considering all that each had gone through. He said he thought Rob was as stable as he was the first time around since he knew a little more about what to expect and the experiences he had to his advantage. He wished him every bit of good fortune possible and he would expect him to see him first as soon as he gets back. Rob thanked him for all that he had done to keep him on the right path.

Rob had lunch at the commissary and asked if he could speak to the chef who came out and said how glad he was to meet Rob. Rob said he just wanted to compliment him and his staff on all of the good food he had been able to enjoy every time he had been to NASA. The chef said they were proud to have been a part of the teleportation and they would be looking forward to his return to be of service again.

Rob made his way to Sarah's office but he was not looking forward to the encounter.

The first thing she said was, "Have you been trying to ignore me Dr. Roby?" to which he replied "A little maybe, kinda, sorta…"

"Well at least you're honest, what's going on?"

"It's just…"

"Never mind, I know."

"You do?"

"Duh…it's obvious you are not interested."

"Then you don't know…that is NOT 'it' at all."

"Well what is 'it' then?"

"The fact of the matter is I can't let you, or me, get involved at a level of extreme anguish if I don't make it back."

"Don't you talk that way or even think that is a possibility."

125

"But..."

"No but's, if's or even maybe's, you are coming back and I want to be a part of your life."

"But I'm an old man, well maybe just older, and you have a long, wonderful, promising life ahead of you and you don't need to be spending any part of it taking care of an old broke-down archaeologist."

With that she kissed him and said, "What if I don't want to spend it with anyone else?"

At that moment nothing else, not all the admonitions, cautions, warnings or reticence mattered, he couldn't suppress his feelings any longer and kissed her deeply.

They held each other a long time and when she started to say something he said, "We can't make any commitments, at least not now, because what I am about to embark on is extremely dangerous and the chances of my successful return are very slim, trust me because I know whereof I speak and I cannot let you make any pledges or sacrifices planning on my homecoming."

With that she started to cry and finally said, "My head tells me you are right but my heart is breaking...I want to be with you and prove my love."

"You don't have to prove anything...I know that, but as much as I need you right now I would be thinking about you constantly and that singular frame of mind might mean the difference between life or death."

"I never thought of it from that standpoint, I was being selfish, I'm sorry."

"Don't ever be sorry for loving someone, especially if you find someone or someone finds you in my absence, you grab onto it and hold onto it and make it last, it will only get better with age, but, if I do make it back in one piece and you are still around I will come a-courting."

"Don't you count me out, I'm a pretty damned determined woman and I'll hold you to it...now get out of here before I change my mind and take you down."

Rob said, "Yes ma'am" and she just smiled and hugged him tightly.

While he was positive he had done the right thing, he had many normal regrets but surprisingly he didn't feel guilty. Somehow he now knew Della would want him to go on with his life and have someone in his life to share these new experiences and be with him when he needed support and comfort and love. He spent the evening writing in his journal about all of the complicated issues, occurrences and circumstances that he had experienced over the last few hours which helped immensely confront the challenges he was facing in the coming hours.

He got to Baker's office early and met him as he arrived at his office. Fortunately, there were no requirements prior to this physical. However, they did double check everything that had been done previously and it was time consuming, with a new set of practitioners asking the same questions and redoing all of the standard evaluations and dutifully recording the results, Rob guessed for comparative purposes. The exams took all morning and Baker said he would go over everything that afternoon but he didn't see any reason not to plan on proceeding with the mission and to take it easy before the "lift off".

Sarah was waiting in the foyer as he came out. She said, "Can I at least buy you lunch?" Rob said, "Sure."

She took them in her car to a nice seafood restaurant and they decided to split a large red snapper with all the trimmings. She was quite conciliatory and apologized about coming on so strong and that she understood and appreciated his mature approach to their relationship. She also admitted to being attracted to his media persona at first but how much she admired his true, honest character and that the feelings she expressed were genuine. Rob expressed his appreciation for her understanding and reiterated his interest, all things being the same when he returned, carefully avoiding the "if" possibility.

She had some good observations about the landscape they had surveyed and the rest of their time together went well. She took Rob back to Baker's office and said she was not going to say, "Goodbye", just that she would see him when he got back and kissed him on the cheek. Rob could see the tears in her eyes and said simply, "See you then."

Baker's report was mostly positive, with the only admonitions centering around his aging body that would be subjected to all the obvious stresses it was going to be forced to endure. AND that he would pay for it when he returned. Rob acknowledged the challenges and thanked him for his concern and compassion. Baker ended by saying he would expect Rob to be at the teleportation facility by 6 PM the next day.

He didn't feel like eating much that evening and just ordered a toasted cheese sandwich and chips. He skyped Nita that night and told her how much he loved her and that he would see her at NASA in exactly a year. He could tell she was crying and repeated that he **would** see her in a year.

He had the breakfast buffet the next morning and spent the better part of the day writing in his journal his final thoughts just in case something happens to prevent his return. It was mostly thanking all who believed in the project and helped him fulfill his dream to learn about the people who lived during the first settlement of the Americas as well as his hope that what he had participated in is just the first step in understanding the past for the betterment of those living today and into the future. This was also the time he missed Della the most, she was with him during the last few hours before his last translocation and they had shared some intimate, memorable moments and he missed that and her greatly.

# Chapter 11

## "Lift Off" and New Encounters

He got to the round building at 6 PM and they began the preparation for his departure and once again it appeared as if everyone was excited about the event and everyone he had been meeting with was there to wish him well, except Sarah and that was OK with him since he didn't want her to see him necked, at this point anyway. Ellis reminded him that if he didn't make it to Lindenmeier they would try Alibates as well, just in case he was closer to the drop site.

The time came for the final wipe down and send off scheduled for 9 PM. There was a hush and then the anesthesia feeling and he was back at Alibates. Same place, but a very different time, it was cold, at least colder than he had experienced during the Clovis Period. He saw no campfires and fortunately there was about a half moon and he could see to make his way to the shelter he and the Young Woman had used previously. It helped to get in out of the wind and as he was trying to scoop out a place to lie down he found something totally unexpected. The Young Woman had carefully buried all of his belongings in the driest portion of the shelter! This was an incredible, powerful, unbelievable, experience and a connection with another individual in his life he could never have expected. Even though 1500 years separated them he couldn't help but be overwhelmed and he cried.

The dryness of the deposit preserved everything extremely well just has it did in the in the rock shelters he had visited in southwest Texas where even fiber artifacts survived. He would have to wait until morning to determine how much of the material was usable but this could be an enormous advantage in his survival during the initial stages of his second journey. He was able to shake out the robe which had lost most of its hair and was stiff but still was a welcome cover for the rest of the night. His thoughts went back to the Young Woman and what had happened to her, it made sense that she could not have carried everything with her but her careful preservation of his personal items certainly demonstrated her affection for him. Rest was difficult with an overload of new thoughts but as daylight illuminated the space he dug deeper and found his atlatl, possibles bag with the hammerstone, billet, foreshafts, knapped points and knives and even the lion claw. Rats had chewed a hole in the bag and all of the tanned hide items were stiff but with some work almost everything would be salvageable. The cane darts were no longer useable all the sinew would have to be replaced on most of the sewn pieces but what a testament to the Young Woman! Maybe somehow, in some way she thought he might return and she knew he would come back to this spot, or perhaps it was just a memorial, a remembrance of their time together. The only thing missing was his date staff/spear. She must have taken it and that pleased him immensely. Did she ever come back to see if he had returned? Did she have a fulfilling life? Rob was appreciative of her in the past and even more so now.

As he surveyed the landscape he could certainly discern some changes. A lot, if not most of the larger trees were gone, replaced with a greater number of juniper and not nearly as many varieties of ground cover or as much grass. The Canadian River was stable but not as much flow as he had seen in his last trip. While he had his Paleo clothes he needed some lanolin from some source to work in and soften the leather goods and he didn't think he could collect enough rabbit brains to do much good. There were some hoof prints along the edge of the water but too old to be distinguishable. He made his way up to the quarries and could tell there had been a lot more activity in intervening years with numerous pits dug to extract the flint but no signs of recent excavations. He was able to rub some of the rawhide string between his hands and soften it enough to make a couple of rabbit snares and set them out.

He was sure if it was this much cooler it was going to be very cold during the winter and he would need more protection as well as a lot of jerky and other provisions but for now he would stay in the shelter and scout for larger game and additional potential food resources.

He remembered he and the Young Woman had found some deer in a tributary running into the river basin to the west and ventured in that direction that afternoon. He found a doe and a new fawn but did not disturb them and began seeking a source for making some darts. There was a large dead pecan tree about a mile upriver and a few straight limbs remaining and he cut a couple of shafts that with a great deal of smoothing might work. The wood was hard and brittle and would probably only be good for one try so he would have to be sure of his shot. One of the pieces was solid enough to make his calendar staff and while it would take some time and effort to work it down to the heart wood it would be substantial enough to serve as a good spear as well.

He went back to the shelter and checked his snares, fortunately he had caught a rabbit. He reset the trap and gathered some wood, built a fire and skinned and spitted the creature with gratitude for its nourishment. He worked on the shafts by fire light until late that night and was finally satisifed with the results. He tied the two smallest Clovis points to the foreshafts with some sinew from the rabbit and felt confident that the reconditioned rig would work...at least once.

He slept well, realizing that all of his energies that day, both physical and mental, had gone into his new life...as it should for the next year. His physical "restoration" was not as dramatic as before but he did feel good however, he had aged some and the new revitalization may be from the excitement of being "back".

He woke early and made his way to where he had seen the deer. There was, as his colleagues, and his research predicted, a strong westerly wind which will probably be the norm for this time period. His approach was carefully planned and he found the pair laying down near some dead trees, too old to tell what kind, but with the wind in his favor he was able to get within 20 yards without being detected. The only shot was at the doe's back which, dependent on his accurcy, would be fatal and prevent her from running off.

She sensed the movement of his arm casting the dart but it was too late, the projectile point entered between the vertrebre and severed the spinal cord. The fawn ran a few yards and bleated but confused it just stood there and although it would normally be against Rob's nature he used the second dart to put it down too. He knew it was too young to make it on its own and his survival had no qualms.

He dressed out the two animals quickly skinning both and quartering the doe, taking the whole fawn and the backstraps back to the shelter. He made quick work of the fawn making jerky meat and hanging it up on a makeshift pole for the time being. He went back after the hides, livers, hearts and another quarter and a final trip to get the two front quarters and put the brains in the doe's bladder. He hung everything from a large limb on a dead cottonwood tree just down the slope from the shelter and cooked the heart and liver of the fawn. It was good, very mild tasting and filling. He streched out the hides on the limestone above the shelter as he had done in a previous time and began to cut up the doe into strips to add to the jerky pole. It would be a restful night as his thoughts turned to processing the rest of the meat and knapping some points as soon as he could.

The next few days were busy trying to take advantage of the cool, clear weather preparing the jerky, making Midland-like, actually more Plainview-like points and working the brains into his old clothing. It went well and after a lot of smoothing over a limb of the cottonwood the leather became, while not soft, at least pliable. He knew he looked like he had seen much better days, even scruffy, but at least the pieces covered his private parts and helped keep the wind off of most of his body and it would give him some time to come up with a better and more comfortable solution.

He ate some of the other heart and liver as well as some of the backstrap and caught a couple of more rabbits and felt he had enough provisions to begin his trek toward Lindenmeier. While he had not tanned the hides he had scraped the flesh side and prepared them for future use. He cleaned out the doe's bladder for water storage and made the doe's skin into a knap sack to carry the jerky.

According to his staff he had marked his 12th day in the Folsom Period and was thankful for his good fortune this time around as well. As he started upstream to the west he tried to stay in the river bottom as much as he could exiting only when he had to because it was very rough going trying to cross the many draws and ravines coming into the main drainage system. He was making good time but could tell the land was still in a drought as they thought it would be at the end of the Pleistocene and at the beginning of the Holocene and if they were correct in their evaluations of the Younger Dryas the majority of the megafauna had become extinct. He hadn't even seen another mammal at the point where he thought he was crossing the future state line from Texas into New Mexico. He had been able to spear a few perch in some of the larger pools in the river but there were fewer avain species than he had seen during the Clovis Period, mostly just Meadow Larks, Horned Larks, sparrows, ravens, hawks and vultures.

By the time he got to Ute Creek he reaffirmed the comparison they had made during the fly over, that if it was dry or just a trickle during modern times that would be what he would find during the Folsom Period. Sure enough, there was only a minimal amount of water flowing into the Canadian and it would not be a dependable source if he tried to follow it northward to the Folsom Type Site. He did see some deer tracks leading upstream along the creek bank but since he still had a good supply of jerky he did not expend his time in trying to hunt them down. He often wished for some of the seasoning, especially salt, the Young Woman had in the pouch she carried with her.

Rob's energy level was still good and he was traveling at least 10 miles a day but knew he would need some vegetable sustinance soon.

He got into a sand dune biome further up the Canadian and found some deep hollows with large cottonwoods and oaks. He started to see some coyotes and a bobcat as well as lots of mice, rabbits and deer sign.

As he topped one of the tallest dunes he thought he saw a person going over another dune about a mile away. He picked up his pace and did his best to catch up to see if he really had seen another human. By the time he got to where he thought he had seen someone, sure enough there were human tracks headed west but he couldn't see the individual. He followed the tracks and gradually the dune field changed to hard gound and that's when he saw the group. About 10-12 people walking directly away from him at a fast clip now about half a mile in the distance. He decided not to holler at them so he could maintain his silence if they let him join them. One of the group looked back and they picked up their stride in an obvious move to leave him behind.

Had they seen him earlier without his noticing? Did he appear to be a threat in some way? Were they afraid of any outsider? He could probably find them by nightfall but should he try?

They were probably headed for the Estancita Basin where numerous Folsom sites had been recorded and there would likely be a salt source. It would also be a lot closer for him rather than trying to get to Lindenmeier, however, a major site like Lindenmeier had not been found there. He sat down on top of the nearest dune and comtemplated his options...he could certainly make it back to Alibates in a year, he knew the route well now, but his objective was to live with these people for as long as he could before his return. His contact with the group he had just encountered, in all likelihood, would now be perceived as agression on his part and he did not want to create a confrontational situation that could end badly.

From his position he could see where the Canadian turned north and convinced himself that he should continue on to the original goal.

He didn't make camp until dark, a good piece up the river from where he had seen the Folsom people thinking it was possible that the group might send some of the young men back to check him out and he didn't want to take a chance on their motives if they did.

He didn't build a fire and kept his weapons close just in case…it was a long night. He was able to get up on a ridge the next morning and didn't see any other humans so he was pretty sure they had not tried to follow him.

It wouldn't be long until he entered the southern end of the Canadian River canyon. This would be the first major challenge to his physical abilites. It was deep, with walls reaching over 300 feet above the river and rugged beyond human capabilities, at least older humans like him. Even if he stayed in the bottom along the river there were huge boulders that would prevent any reasonable progress on foot. So as he had determined during the fly over he would have to get up on the rim of the canyon, probably on the west side as there appeared to be more potential water sources available along that escarpment.

Somewhere near where Logan, New Mexico is today he exited the canyon but it didn't take long to see that all the drainages coming into the Canadian on the west side were deep and wide making it very difficult to transverse but he could see the other side was mostly flat plains and the few draws flowing toward the canyon were much more managable. It might mean that he would have to desend down into the canyon on occasion to be able to get water but he would be able to advance along this stretch a lot quicker in the long run.

He had to go back down and up the other side before it got worse and in the process ran into a small herd of bachelor bucks, they were mule deer, the first he had seen and they didn't seem scared. He was able to take a shot before they fled but his dart was much lighter with the Midland-like point and it flew over its target. A clean miss! The point and dart shattered. He was greatly disappointed. He could have used the hide and it would have resupplied his food reserves. He followed them up the canyon thinking they might get that curious again but to no avail. As he got to the top of the east side he began to see herds of Pronghorn, the same species he had hunted in Colorado but it was getting late and he really perferred the hide of a deer or bison for the tanning process, beside the fact that Pronghorn would be the most elusive game animals he could hunt.

He was able to make good time along the eastern rim of the canyon and continued to see small herds of deer and Pronghorn but the deer moved quickly down into the edge of the canyon and the Pronghorns were not letting him get within range of a kill.

He found what looked like a sensible place to make his way down to get some fresh water and about half way to the bottom he could see some deer lying down with their backs to him facing the wind. He was above them and carefully worked around so he could take a shot. The closest to him was a large buck still in velvet, as he cast the dart the buck sensed the movement and stood up but instead of hitting it in the back he caught it right behind the shoulder. It made a couple of jumps and stumbled and fell. The pleasure of his success was quickly quelled as he realized how difficult it would be to get the animal out of the canyon. It was very steep and rocky and it would take a lot of energy and fortitude to salvage the harvest. After gutting it he was able to drag it to a more level spot and skinned it out and began quartering it. By then he needed water and went on down to the river. He saw lots of fish in the larger pools but didn't fool with them at this point. He went back up and got the hide, backstraps, heart and liver and tried to carry one of the hind quarters but it was too much trying to get back up the cliff. He went back down and got one of the fore quarters and it was all he could do to get it back to his camp. It was getting dark so he decided to take a chance on leaving the rest until morning. He fixed some of the heart and liver which was strong but it was good to have fresh meat. He staked out the hide so it would dry some before he scraped it. He was thinking about leaving the hair on it and just tan the flesh side so as not to take as long but he really needed to make some new clothes, he would have to see how it played out.

The next morning was cloudy and looked like rain, more so than at any-time since he had been on this journey. As he got back to the kill site he saw coyotes running away. They had eaten most of one of the hind quarters and all of one of the other front quarter. Fortunately they had not chewed into the skull because he needed the brains to tan the hide.

He was able to salvage the deer bladder and broke open the skull and got the brains. He was able to carry what was remaining of the hind quarter but decided to leave the other front quarter the coyotes had chewed on so they would stay away from his campsite.

By late morning it started to rain and by his calendar staff it was the second of July, the beginning of the monsoon season but more importantly his and Della's wedding anniversary. He didn't have time to dwell on that at the moment as he was trying to put together a brush arbor to protect all of his possessions. It took a lot of work because all that was in the immediate vicinity was juniper trees and it took a lot of limbs to stave off the downpour.

That night he was melancholy with many memories of their lives together and it would be with him a lot over the next few days. He was able to save all of his provisions and as it cleared the next morning he began in earnest to start preparing the jerky and initiate the tanning process. It was a good hide so he decided to dedicate whatever time necessary to make his new clothing and utilize the old material for some new moccasins. He didn't have enough to make a new possibles bag and not enough brains to work into the first two deer hides he had brought with him but what he was accomplishing would be a welcome change.

It took a little over a week to complete all of his projects but it went well and he was proud of the results and needed the rest before trying to finish the canyon route and head for the Folsom Type Site.

The rest of that part of the endurance went well. He saw more deer and Pronghorn and some elk on the western side of the canyon which was encouraging. He continued to see coyotes, a mountain lion and even a pair of wolves but they they were the modern species not the Dire Wolves he had encountered during the Clovis Period and they kept their distance. With the two bladders he was able to go much further without going back down into the canyon which saved a lot of time and energy. There were more showers but there were also larger trees, both pines and cottonwoods especially where there were some small water impoundments, not as big as lakes but cerainly good sized ponds. He was able to get some frogs and cattail tubers and a few small turtles. The change in his food resources seemed to energize him and he made into the low rolling plains where the going was much easier.

As he got close to where Springer, New Mexico is in modern times he began to encounter lots of berries and Pinon trees and was able to gather a good supply of Pinon nuts.

Due to the rains he was confident that the next leg of his venture would be manageable because even during the fly over he saw tinajas with water in them and there should be a plentiful supply at this time of the year as well.

He could clearly see the mountains to the west now and knew there had been Folsom sites found in the tributaries running down from their eastern edges but by his calculations he couldn't expend any additional time hunting for the humans and should stay on course.

He started to recognize some of the landmarks he has seen driving through the area when he was a grad student, but he couldn't make out Capulin Volcano yet which would be the key to finding the Folsom Type Site.

As he cut northeastward across the hills and valleys he did find numerous tinajas with good water and began to see more Pronghorn, deer and a few herds of elk. The larger predators were gone as were the species he found common during the Clovis Period. No camels, horses, peccary, four-horned antelope and of course mammoths but he hopefully will encounter the last of the giant bison at some point.

About half way to Capulin he could make out the cone that is so prominent in the region. He also encountered an ideal stalking situation when he found some elk lying down out of the wind against a small rise. They hadn't seen him and he was able to circle around them and get the wind in his favor and sneek to within about 35 yards of a cow. His only shot was at her back and with the wind blowing as much as it was it was chancy but he really did need a new robe. As he let fly all she did was turn her head but he hit her pretty far back and she was still able to frail with her front legs. He ran down to cut her throat and in the melee one of her hooves hit Rob in the head. When he came to his senses he felt blood running down his face. The elk was dead a few yards away but he had a bad scalp wound and it was hurting like hell. He washed his face and the cut she had created but it wasn't too severe, just a lot of blood and a bad headache.

He was going to need a few days to recover anyway which would give him time to process the animal and tan the hide.

He left the hair on during this proceedure and it would make a good robe to keep him warm in the coming months. His knap sack was full and he had three bladders for water but it was a load that would lighten as he progressed.

He skirted the western side of Capulin and found Wild Horse Arroyo but couldn't find the Folsom Type Site at least where the bison were killed and butchered around 11,000 years ago. It probably hadn't happened yet or the evidence was covered up by recent geological episodes. He was now in the headwaters of the Cimmaron River and was seeing deer, elk and Pronghorn on the plains below.

He made his way to where Sarah had seen a good crossing over the rough ridges into what was to become Colorado. It was probably Trinchera Pass where Charles Goodnight, after Oliver Loving's untimely death, had taken as many a 2,000 head of Longhorns at a time into northeastern Colorado to sell to John Wesley Illif who bought as many as 10,000 head over a three year period. From the pinnacle he could make out the drainages into the Purgatory River and began to make his way down into his home state which he knew well. He could begin to see mountains to the west, the Spanish Peaks and a portion of the Sangre de Cristos. It was still dry but not dissimilar to modern times and he knew there would be game where there was water.

When he got to the Purgatory he found small catfish and perch in the pools and took advantage of a few. It was easy following the river bottom which had willows, cottonwoods, reeds and some berry vines. He was able to make some good dart shafts and had the luxury of making some practice casts into the soft bank. He still had a good food supply but did not know what he was going to encounter at the Arkansas or beyond so he couldn't tarry. He had hunted pheasants, prairie chickens, Pronghorns and white-tailed deer in the vacinity and was able to recognize a few prominent landmarks. It was August and it got hot during the days, but it was enjoyable, this part of the trip was timeless as though he could be there back then or now.

Not far from where the Purgatory runs into the Arkansas he could see a major storm in the headwaters of the Purgatory but he thought any increase in the flow would be hours away. He was wrong. He could hear the roar of the flash flood and barely made it out of the bottom before it engulfed the whole valley. He did have the foresight to exit on the west side of the event so he would be able to work his way upstream of the Arkansas because it could been many days before he could cross either river if he had been on the other side.

It was still a formidable challenge, the flow from the Purgatory was backing up the Arkansas and it was wide, swift and deep so his only alternative was to follow it west until he could find a safe crossing. He remembered a potential place at what eventually became Bent's Fort where the Santa Fe Trail crossed so he made his way to that junctor. He could see where the water had been higher but it was receeding so he decided to wait a day or two and let it go down a little more. It was a relaxing time as he rested and enjoyed the shade of the big cottonwoods. There were lots of birds, blackbirds, swallows, sparrows, raptors and even a few ducks with little ones.

The Arkansas was clear as a crystal and it even smelled fresh unlike the same river of modern times that had become dingy and had a rusty odor. He reflected on how much things had changed even in his lifetime, the air, the water, the land and what his generation was still doing or actually not doing to prevent futher degradation or at the very least stabilize the assult on future generations. He pledged outloud that he would be more of an advocate upon his return to protect the only environment surviving the progress of humanity.

But he had to get on his way so he wrapped up everything in two bundles and carefully made his way across the river. It was still swift but he was able to control his footing and made the second trip without incident.

Having conquered the most difficult geographic obstacles he and his colleagues had predicted he would face he was feeling good about the rest of the journey, however, winter was coming and that might be the biggest challenge yet.

# Chapter 12
# The Last Leg

There it was! A human footprint! It was on the north side of the river and was old, at least several days, maybe a week, in the mud and laking distinction and enough detail to determine exact size, but there it was. After searching extensively he could neither find additional numbers of individuals or where the person was headed, only pointing westerward up river. What was a single individual without the protection of their group doing in such an isolated place? The river would be a logical passage from one location to another but from where to what objective? Did he or she see him and advoid contact? Would he have been perceived as a threat and why? It was perplexing and very disappointing that he had been so close to an encounter with a Folsom person and not being able to interact.

Knowing the terrain he headed due north because he knew he would get to Horse Creek that ran into the Arkansas from the northwest. It was easy going and he made it in good shape. He could now see Pikes Peak to the west and it already had some snow on top of it and the nights were getting nippie even though the days were perfect. It was hard to beat fall in Colorado even during the Folsom Period.

As he left the upper end of Horse Creek trecking toward the landscape that led into Beaver Creek he could tell the wind was getting stronger than anything he had encounterd thus far in either expedition. He could also tell there was a major sandstorm looming in the southwest and approaching at a swiftness that made him fear the possible consequences.

He was in the open plains with no shallowness in the geography that he could see from his vantage point. He had to make a decision quickly, because depending on its duration it could challenge his survival. He stuck his staff as far into the ground as he was capable and wrapped his older hide around it getting inside with his belongings just as the sand started stinging his flesh. He has been in sandstorms in New Mexico in his younger years that took the paint off of his front license plate but that was going into the wind at 60 miles an hour. This seemed to be at least hurricane force wind and was carrying larger grains of quartz sand that pierced and bit into everything that was exposed. Even in his makeshift shelter he had to use the smaller robe to cover his crouched body. The fine dust filtered in and made breathing difficult but there was no way he could risk rearranging the protective coverings to his advantage…he just had to hang on, literally to his possessions. The storm had hit in the early afternoon and its strength went unabated well into the night enough to become dangerous to his breathing abilities. When it finally passed he was able to make a cold camp and eat some jerky and drink some water and get a little rest. He felt most fortunate that he still had his senses intact enough to survive that environmental impact.

He began to encounter some shallow draws that would lead to the headwaters of Beaver Creek and while was still making good time and feeling well a freak snow storm hit late one afternoon and it was all he could do to find some shelter along the bank of a tributary running into Bijou Creek. It wasn't the most desirable refuge but it was out of the brunt of the wind and he was able to cover himself and his belongings with his robe and the old hide that had a now shiney apparance on the outside from the sandblasting. Fortunately it was over by morning and it was clear and calm and the snow would melt quickly but it was apparent that he needed better foot coverings as this was only the beginning of a most undesirable winter if he couldn't find or actually make something better for his feet. He guessed he was just getting older because he hadn't noticed the cold as much in the Clovis Period.

He was getting low on jerky and needed to take advantage of the next opportunity to harvest some game but luck was not with him and it made him realize how fortunate he had been until now. He made his way on down Bijou Creek and when he got close enough to discern the confluence with the South Platte River he could see bison, a substantial herd of about 30. They didn't appear as large as the giant bison he had hunted in the Clovis Period more like the buffalo that had innudated the Great Plains in modern times. The problem was that everything was against the hunter, wind direction, they could see for miles and no way to utilize the landscape for a stalk. They were not particularly wary and were just feeding on the north side of the river and he thought about making a cold camp but there was frost in the mornings now and he needed the warmth of a fire during the night. So he gathered some wood and built a fire out of sight of the herd but he knew the smoke would drift in their direction. Sure enough they were gone by sunrise and the wind was still not condusive to trying to follow them up. He was now only about 50 miles from Lindenmeier and even though those were the first bison he had seen he considered it a better use of his time at this stage to travel on to his destination. He was able to catch some rabbits in snares as his larder got lower but the big game was eluding him.

As he got to the headwaters of the South Platte he began to see lots of deer, elk and bison sign and he was getting into an edge habitat with pines jutting out onto the plains...good for the hunter. There was light snow falling and covering the ground and tracking was easy. He set his sights on the bison tracks and finally caught the wind right so his stealth was enhanced by the elements. He found a small group of cows and calves standing in a small opening in the pines on a hillside above a creek running eastward toward the river. He had several animals to choose from and being undetected he picked a large cow about 30 yards away. His dart found the vitals and they all bolted in a dead run trying to escape from whatever caused the panic. The cow made it about 100 yards before going down. He quickly gutted her and proped open the body cavity and slit the throat open to cool. His first thought was that this would put him in good standing with the people at Lindemeier but he would have to bring them back to the kill site because he couldn't pack but a small portion of the animal on his initial encounter.

It was mid-morning and if he pushed it he might reach the campsite by late afternoon. He took the heart and liver and some hump meat in his new robe, his atlatl and a few darts and some water, leaving the rest of his gear in the body cavity hoping that might deter predators from trying to scavenge the kill. He also pulled the gut pile further away so anything desiring to take advantage of the opportunity might be more likely to concentrate on it until he could get back.

He set out in a fast walk and kept to the edge of the forest so he could look for the hill he had identified on the fly over and where the helicopter pilot had landed.

A little after noon he could see the destination and he could see a small plume of smoke. Folsom people! He took a moment to savor the scene and the accomplishment of all that had led up to this point.

As he approached the camp he could see only a couple of structues, hide draped but more sophisticated than those of the Clovis people. There were several women and a few young girls but no men or boys. He guessed they were on a hunting expedition but he caused a great deal of commotion creating an obvious fearful situation for them. He held out the heart and liver as an offering which calmed the older women and two of them came over to look at him but did not accept the presentation. It took a few uneasy moments of curiosity to overcome their hesitancy but one took the heart and the other took the liver. Rob then pulled out the hump meat and some of the younger women ran over and grabbed it out of his hands. He then motioned for them to follow him and he turned to retrace his foot prints but they didn't follow and began talking among themselves Finally the two older women came over and started talking to him and he quickly pointed to his ears and shook his head negatively. They then went back to the group and conversed at length, probably about his apparence and disability. He could sense an atmosphere of fear and he could understand that to some degree but he hoped their need for fresh meat would overcome their indecision. Knowing this could go on for a lengthly period he motioned again for them to follow him and finally the two older women and two of the young women gathered their robes, possibles bags and some water and started after him.

Rob knew they would have to hurry to get there by sunset but not only were they keeping up they were pushing him to his limits. They seemed to be very pleased with the bounty and immediately built a fire and began skinning and butchering with each one putting about 50 pounds of meat in their robes. They then built the fire all the way around the kill and they all headed back to the campsite. Rob was only able to carry his personal gear and a back strap. The women talked all the way back and the group was enthusatically received when they arrived. It was probably close to midnight but they started roasting the backstrap and some of the liver and heart. It was all Rob could do to stay awake...it had been a long trip and a very long day and he was exhausted but he did enjoy the meal which had some of the same kind of seasoning the Young Woman from the Clovis Period used. They put him in one of the shelters and all the others squeezed into the other one. He could hear them chattering for a good while but it didn't take long for him to have the best sleep he had been afforded since his arrival back to the Folsom era.

He was awakened the next morning by a commotion, as he went out he saw two of the young women arguing but he couldn't determine what it was about. The women already had a meal ready which consisted of a soup made from some of the contents of the intestines. It was strong but the seasoning made it palatable. All but the girls and one of the young women who was in the heated disagreement started out with Rob to finish the retrieval of the kill. Rob suspected the argument was over which one would stay with the girls or maybe it was about not being able to sleep in her shelter. There were still coals around the bison and it had not been scavanged but all of the innerds had been eaten or dragged off. When Rob looked at the tracks it was definitely wolves but not as big as the Dire wolves from the Clovis Period. The women made short work of the job at hand and they were ready to head back by noon. It was all Rob could do to carry the skull and hide but each of the women had just as big a load as he did. He was able to take a humerus for his futue foreshafts and was surprised they didn't take more of the bone for marrow and tools.

They quickly set about making jerky and roasting large pieces of meat for the evening meal which he enjoyed but he did not want to be the cause of internal strife so he retrieved his belongings and made his way down into a shallow revine and built a fire and set up a sparce encampment using his old robe as a lean-to and covering himself with the new one. He could hear the women talking into the night but he needed more rest which finally came. By the time he woke they had some more soup ready. He was glad that might be all of it but he wasn't about to complain. They already had the hide staked out and were scraping it, the two older women teaching the young girls how to do it properly. Two of the young women returned to camp carrying the long bones from the bison kill and they began splitting them and taking out the marrow for future use.

Because of all of the activity over the last few hours Rob realized he had not marked his calendar staff for the past two days. As he did, he had to do a quick recount to be sure but the day before had been his birthday. But since it had already occurred there was little reason to dwell on it or even contemplate any perspective about his becoming antiquitated.

Rob was finally able to observe the female unit. There were the two older women who would be considered middle age by modern standards probably a little over 35 years old. There were three young women who were probably daughters of the older women and four children that were probably the younger women's kids. They all looked a lot like the Young Woman from the Clovis Period with reddish brown hair, caucasoid features and a weathered complection as a result of exposure to the elements throughout their lifetimes. Their clothing was much more accomplished than that of the Young Woman, their tops and skirts were well tanned and the moccasins had rounded toes and everything was tightly sewn. They were perhaps much more serious and were not demonstrable in any sense of the meaning. Finally Rob went over to the two older women and pointed to himself and made a sweeping motion with his hand and shrugged his shoulders. They talked a minute in a language that Rob thought sounded a little like, a few words anyway, Iroquoian based on what he had listened to after conferring with George once he returned from his first venture back in time. One of them then shrugged her shoulders. Rob thinking they couldn't or didn't understand his question of where were the men in the group just hung his head trying to think of another way to express his concern. Then one of the women placed her hand on his chest and shook her head negatively. Rob held out his hands and shrugged again. They both made jesters of death and burial. Was this the beginning of the end of these people, had the onslaught of the peopling of the New World from Beringia becoming the reason for their demise? It would stand to reason that the males in an attempt to protect the population would have placed themselves in harm's way and been the first to die. But what of the women, like this group, who still survive? Are they just not considered a threat or they look different, sound different, smell different and are not desirable for mating or even slave purposes? Whatever the reason, Rob had already negated his pledge to not interfere in any way by sharing the bison kill with them and he probably will continue to help them in the immediate furture in order to provide for his own needs.

It was getting complicated, by any measure, one of his primary objectives was to see how the group, families and outsiders interacted but this was far from normal and Rob became concerned on another level. What if some of the new people came into the area and found him? What would be their reaction? He had little choice since he had to be at this location when the time came so he was now in the do or die corner.

Life settled into a routine, the women had used his bison hide, a hide they had and his old hide as a flap for a small but comfortable place for him to stay in which they set up not far from their structures. He went out hunting on a regular basis and was able to supply some small game, a yearling bison and a young bull elk. He saw a grizzly bear but gave it a wide berth not wanting an encounter of a questionable ending without other hunters backing him up. The Young Woman from the Clovis experience seemed to be the exception as none of the women with whom he was sharing the campsite ever offered to go with him or, since he had been there anyway, gone out on their own with an atlatl and darts. They were very frugal in their use of their food reserves making mostly soups in the same way the Clovis people did, with various substances added, some of which Rob couldn't identify, but all seemingly nourishing.

Snow was getting deep in the mountains but Lindenmeier was somewhat protected and the snow melted regularly. Rob had made some moccasins from the new elk hide from a pattern he remembered using in his old Boy Scout days and they were working well. He noted Christmas and longed for his other life...both in the far away past as well as what the future might hold and thoughts of Sarah.

# Chapter 13

## Outsiders and Back Again

One afternoon just as spring began to flourish, five individuals appeared on the hill overlooking the campsite that Rob had selected for his extraction back to NASA. It looked to be three adult males and two teenage boys. It was hard to distinguish details but they appeared to be of the Mongoloid race. Long straight black hair, slender build and much darker skin pigmentation. They stayed a good while, fortunately the women did not see them so Rob acted like he was intent on doing something with his darts. He could tell there was a great deal of discussion, sometimes animated, which was probably about his presence in the group since they had not bothered the women thus far. They disappeared as quickly as they had come and Rob hoped that they had decided that an old man was not a challenge to their occupation of the region. However, he kept his weaponary in hand just in case…he was not going to let them take him captive or kill him if he could prevent it…damn the commitments not to interfere with the past or future if it meant defending his life.

He did not see them again during the next few days but he did find out what they were looking for…bison…great numbers of them returning from the south. He was able to find a small group of cows and yearlings in a draw not far from camp and was able to bring down an old cow. She was big and would supply a lot of meat for the foreseeable future and a great robe for the women. Once again the women made quick work of all the preparations necessary to utilize the animal as a food and protective resource.

Just before he was to be transported he went up to the top of the hill and confirmed exactly where he would sit and looked at the surroundings one more time with more regrets than answers. He had learned a lot but not what he had hoped for and it was disappointing, not just because he didn't have the social order he sought but also he did not have the reasons for their demise, even genetically, of what happened to the Clovis and Folsom people. More importantly, he would not be able to take back what the next step would be in trying to arrive at some conclusions.

As he started down the backside of the hill to see if it would be a better route coming up in the dark he came face to face with one of the new people. It was an adult male and definitely of the Mongolid race, he was carrying an atlatl and darts but Rob only had his calendar staff with him which probably enhanced his elderly apparance. They stared at each other for what seemed like several minutes, he was dressed similarly but the points on the foreshafts were of the Agate Basin variety, long, collaterally flaked and everything he had with him was a result of fine workmanship. He made no aggressive movements, but he was obviously very curious. However it was probably to Rob's advantage that he had not brought along his weaponery as he, at this point, was no threat to the New Person. The guy did not make any gestures friendly or otherwise and the fellow stalked off around the opposite side of the hill from the campsite, looking back on several occasions while Rob stood his ground.

The encounter was monumental...profound! It made the entire journey, hardships and risks worthwhile. The presence of what would become the Native Americans as they were "discovered" by the Norse, Europeans and Anglos were in direct contact with the Solutrans, or at least, their descendents.

That singular event confirmed the presence of both races in the New World at the same time and that verification was the most significant revolation of his teleportations. The knowledge that at least during this brief period at Lindenmeier there were no males associated with the group Rob had been staying with. The implication, or at least the probability, that the invaders from the north were potentially preventing genetic infilteration was a very real possibility. Even with all of the qualifiers he felt relieved that he would be taking that information back with him. It was what it was and is what it is.

As the day before his departure arrived he made a practice run that night and felt he had everything in order for his return. He did not have the attachment to any of these women he had for the Young Woman and had no personal feelings about the detachment. He was anxious to get home. He was going to leave all of his belongings in his shelter but take a small bag with some of the women's hair that he had picked up from their use of a comb-like object. It was not complicated, just a small simple wooden fork with only about three teeth and while it wasn't used often it seemed to work. This time he felt compelled to take back DNA evidence to help determine their origins and connections to their past.

If he had not been a hunter he probably would not have noticed the movement between the junipers to the south, beyond the draw, but if it was what he thought it was he might be in trouble. He was pretty sure it was a human trying to stay out of sight. That would not be good, as his presence may have convinced others in the party with the man he had encountered on the hill that he was a threat. This would be the most serious challenge he had faced since he began his epic journeys.

He decided to act as though he had not detected the observer and go to his shelter and get his atlatl, quiver and possibles bag as though he was going hunting. He knew that is what they wanted, for him to be alone and vulnerable so this was going to be a cat and mouse, hide and seek game with the disadvantage of having a lot more cats on his tail.

He had gotten to know the area around the campsite quite well and knew some places that he could probably slip their pursuit but it was still unnerving and for the first time he thought, at least considered the possibility that he might not make it back home.

He casually headed northeast along the draw and down toward another deep revine that intersected each other out of sight from where he saw the individual. He then headed northwest up the channel to get into the trees as quickly as possible. This gave him the advantage of looking down on a large area to determine if they were following him.

To his surprise there appeared to be only one person, a young male, who was at the campsite and harrassing the women, making jesters and shouting at them. The women were obviously scared but not understanding his demands. Finally, he headed in the same direction Rob had taken leaving the women shaken but unharmed.

Rob knew The Pursuer would pick up his trail and continue his search. Even though it appeared to be an even match at least, it did not make the situation any more desirable. He agreed with Mike and his other colleagues that he should not change the future of these people reguardles of which population they represented. However, he was determined to protect himself no matter the eventual outcome.

He needed to get to higher ground and stay on a rock path. He knew where he had to go to make a stand in order to have the advantage if a confrontation occurred. It was a difficult path and there was a chance The Pursuer would catch up fast enough to see him trying to avoid an encounter.

As Rob got to a precipice he could see the man still in the bottom of the ravine so that was a relief because he could get to the desired location before The Pursuer could get up to his vantage point.

Rob was able to leave no tracks getting to the box canyon with large boulders he could get behind and then on top of as the cirmstances dictated. That gave him a superior position in case the individual did follow him to that point.

Why was this fellow on a death mission? Either Rob's or his? Was he trying to prove his manhood or was he selected to elininate the last male in the group?

It was starting to get dark which was much to Rob's relief as he would be even harder to detect and was beginning to feel like he would make it after all.

Then he saw him, a lean, well built Asian, taller than the others he had seen and he was scouring the area in an effort to pick up any sign of Rob's presence. He went past the mouth of the box canyon and Rob hoped he would continue on up the mountain or head for his camp, but just as the light faded he came back and headed up the canyon. He was taking it slow, trying to see and even appared to be sniffing the air. Fortunately, it was dead calm and as he got about half way up he stopped and listened. Rob was afraid he would hear his heart beating.

After what seemed like an eternity The Pursuer turned and headed back down the mountain. Rob remained motionless and breathing in silent, shallow breaths. He maintained his position for an hour and then carefully made his way down to the hill where he was to be picked up.

He got there about 8 PM and sat down where they had taken the GPS readings and waited. He was extremely anxious, about to jump out of his skin at every little noise even thought that The Pursuer could have waited for him at the women's camp and heard him summit the hill. He could not recall ever being in a more serious predicament.

He recounted all of his experiences over the past year along with all of the "what if's". What if he had followed the group to the Estancia Valley; what if he had gone over to Ocate, New Mexico near Springer where he had looked at a potentially large Folsom campsite while he was a grad student; he would have still been able to make it back to Alibates; what if he had gone back to Blackwater Draw; what if…there was the same feeling again and he was back! Sitting on the floor with people in white suits wiping him down and taking swabs for analysis and the small container he had made from one of the elk hides with the human hair in it that had also been transported. One of the assistants bagged it for the future studies.

Dr. Baker, was the first to greet him, handing him a hospital gown, asking how he was, to which he replied, "Good, in fact better than you know". Baker said, "We'll see", and took him back to the showers and gave him a towel, washcloth and soap. It was the same joyous renuion with hot water that he had after the last reentry and he took advantage of it for an indeterminable amount of time. There were some scrubs and foot coverings hanging in the shower area so he put them on. Certainly not what he would have had if Della had been there.

Baker met him and took him into an examing room and after a close inspection said he looked good and asked about the new place on his head to which Rob responded, "Encounter with an elk", Baker asked if he needed to know the details and Rob said, "Nope". Baker said they would do all the testing the next morning and he would meet with Dr. Wiley as soon as they got through but right now he knew Rob needed some rest and Deshaun would take him to his room and the chef was waiting up to fix whatever he desired and added that, "everyone would be at the luncheon at Higgin's office tomorrow to welcome him back, oh yeh, your Daughter left word that her flight had been delayed until the next plane departs Munich and won't be here until tomorrow about noon". Rob thanked him and met Deshaun at the entry to the round building.

Deshaun congratulated him on his successful teleportation and said he was glad to be of service to him again. Rob thanked him and said he would see him in the morning and to call him to make sure he was getting ready before he was to pick him up. Deshaun said he would.

His room was exactly as he had left it and he changed into some comfortable clothes and ordered a T-bone and baked potato with a side salad and ice tea. All was good but he was filled with loneliness remembering the home-coming with Della. About the time he finished his meal there was a knock on the door.

It was Sarah holding a bottle of champagne, "Welcome home Dr. Roby".

"Well thank ya, ma'am".

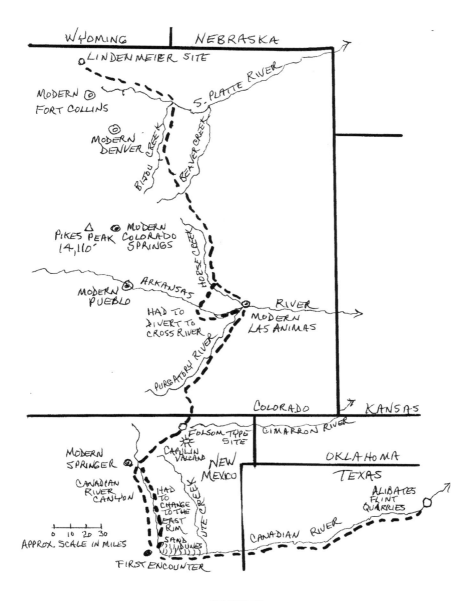

**PART II**

**MAP**

# Part II

# The New Players

**Doug Riggs** – the young archaeologist who Rob thought would be the best person to make the next teleportation back to the Folsom Period but declined due to family obligations.

**Dr. Patrick Higgins** – the new, private contractor and CEO of NASA with a Ph.D. in physics from Stanford, runner-up for the Nobel Prize for his work with the Super Collider during the initial stages while being planned in Texas that was cancelled because it was competing with the budget of NASA at the time.

**Deshaun Taylor** – young aide-de-camp to Dr. Higgins and new host to Rob who had been a student of Dr. Higgins but had proven himself by becoming a successful scientist and researcher in his own right being part of the team who developed the mini solar cells using Nano-technology.

**Dr. Sarah Moore**, dentist, young looking, middle-age, very attractive, who took care of his dental needs before and after Rob's first teleportation becoming attentive and in awe of Rob's experiences with the Paleo people and wanted to go with him on his second translocation. Not able to do that she did get to go on the flight over the proposed route of his new journey and encouraged a serious relationship with him.

**The New Person** – the first one-on-one encounter with an Asian individual that lasted only a few moments but would be remembered the rest of Rob's life

**The Pursuer** – the individual who stalked Rob on his last day of the his second journey

# Glossary

**Agate Basin Point** – A long narrow lanceolate projectile point dating the same time period as Folsom

**Artifact** – An archaeological term referring to anything produced or utilized by humans that remains as evidence of their occupying a particular place during a specific time period.

**Atlatl** – A throwing stick, made with a notch or hook on the end to catch the end of a reed or wooden dart that remained in the hand as the dart was cast giving more leverage and force to the projectile.

**Beringia** – A land bridge occurring across the Bering Strait between what is now Siberia to Alaska when the ice sheets locked up the evaporated water from the oceans dropping the sea level as much as 300' exposing the connecting link between the two continents

**Big blade technology** – In reference to the Clovis culture it is the use of overshot flaking to produce large lithic artifacts that possess a cryptocrystalline structure reduced from flint cores that fracture conchoidally and were made into projectile points, knives, scrapers and other tools.

**Blackwater Draw National Historic Landmark** – An interpretive research center located at the **Clovis Type Site** on **Blackwater Draw** between Clovis and Portales, New Mexico where the first artifacts were found in the 1930's and described the Clovis Points that were in direct association with extinct Columbian mammoths.

**Caucasoid race** – Referring to a grouping of human beings historically regarded as a biologically distinct arising from populations found in Europe, North Africa and western Asia now disputed by anthropologists limiting its use in anthropometry.

**Clovis Period** – Radiocarbon dating of organic materials places the activity of the Clovis occupation based on the distinctive Clovis Points and associated artifacts between 12,900 and 12,500 before the present.

**Clovis Points** – Lanceolate shaped projectile points with fluting typically one third of both surfaces toward the tip of the point with basil smoothing along both edges of the sides equaling the length of the fluting to prevent the securing lashings from being worn. This type of point has been found in and associated with the remains of mammoths and mastodons from the late Pleistocene period.

**Dart** – A straight shaft of either wood or cane usually 6-8 feet in length that is notched in the case of solid wood for the insertion of the projectile point or has a foreshaft that has been notched for insertion of the projectile point and then inserted into the end of the hollow cane each of which has feather fletching and is cast with an atlatl.

**Flint knapping** – The practice of creating flakes from raw material that possess a cryptocrystalline structure struck from cores that fracture conchoidally and are used to make flint blades that then can be knapped using hammerstones, billets and/or antler, bone or wooden flaking tools to produce projectile points, knives, scrapers and other tools.

**Fluting of projectile points** – The act of making a channel or grove on one or both faces of a projectile point as an aid to hafting the point to a wooden shaft or foreshaft. The fluting process required a highly advanced technology typical of the Clovis and Folsom traditions.

**Folsom Period** - Radiocarbon dating of organic materials places the activity of the Folsom occupation based on the distinctive Folsom Points and associated artifacts between 10,900 and 10,200 before the present.

**Folsom Point** – Usually smaller than the Clovis Points the flutes are almost always the entire length of the point and on both sides and are considered one of the finest, most technologically advanced forms of the knapping process. The basil smoothing is often a third of the length of the point toward the tip which is commonly found in and with the remains of the extinct giant bison.

**Folsom Type Site** – Located near the town of Folsom, in northeastern New Mexico on a tributary of the Dry Cimarron River known as Wild Horse Arroyo it was discovered by George McJunkin, a black cowboy and foreman of the Crowfoot Ranch at the beginning of the 20th century. It is considered one of the most historically important archaeological sites in North America because when it was excavated in the 1920's it proved that humans were indeed in direct association with extinct megafauna in the New World having killed giant bison with projectile points that became known as Folsom Points.

**Foreshaft** – A smaller wooden, bone or ivory shaft from 6-24 inches long that is fitted with a projectile point of lithic material, bone, ivory or fire hardened wood which is inserted into a main shaft usually made of the hollow section of a cane or wooden dart.

**Holocene** – The geological and climatological period beginning between 11, 500 and 10,000 years ago and lasting into the present day which was preceded by the Younger Dryas stadial ending the Pleistocene epoch with retreat of the great glaciers and the extinction of up to three quarters of the land mammals in North America.

**Lindenmeier Site National Historic Landmark** – Established on the National Register of Historic Places in 1961 the site was discovered in the 1920's by Judge Claude Coffin, his son Lynn and C. K. Collins and named for the land owner, excavated under the direction of Frank H. H. Roberts from the Smithsonian Institution and John L. Cotter from the then Colorado Museum

of Natural History from 1934-1940. It is considered one of the most important and largest Folsom campsites ever scientifically investigated and the cultural material found has revealed much about the Folsom people.

**Megafauna** – Large animals found at the end of the Pleistocene primary in this reference from 40,000 to 10,000 years ago that succumbed to the changing climate and/or to other forces that caused their extinction including disease and human activity including:

> **American Lions**
> **Bears**
> **Birds – Numerous species**
> **Camels**
> **Dire Wolves**
> **Four-horned Antelope**
> **Giant Armadillos**
> **Giant Beaver**
> **Giant Bison**
> **Giant Tortoise**
> **Horses**
> **Mammoths and Mastodons**
> **Moose**
> **Mountain Deer**
> **Mountain Goat**
> **Muskox**
> **Peccaries**
> **Saber-tooth Cats**
> **Sloths**
> **Tapirs**

**Micro blade technology** – The production of small sharp blades usually from chert, quartz or obsidian that by definition are twice as long as they are wide and can be used for a multiplicity of tools necessary for survival.

**Midland Point** – A projectile point similar to the Folsom Point but without the fluting, thought by some archaeologists to be made from flakes too thin to be fluted or perhaps personal or cultural preference, named from the discovery by Keith "Pat" Glasscock of remains of a human skeleton and distinctive projectile points near Midland, Texas

**Mongoloid race** – A term now considered offensive because of the connotation with Mongolism applied to Down syndrome but originally used to distinguish between Caucasoid, Negroid and the indigenous populations from Asia, eastern Russia, many of the Pacific islands and the Native Americans.

**Pleistocene** – An Epoch that began about 1.8 million years ago and lasted until the beginning of the Younger Dryas and the Holocene approximately 11,700 years ago during the time of continental shifting, major "Ice Ages" with glaciation advances and retreats, sea level fluctuations and many developments and extinctions of animal life including humankind.

**Plainview Point** - Lanceloate shaped projectile points without fluting but typically with some basil thinning of both surfaces toward the tip of the point with basil smoothing along both edges of the sides to prevent the securing lashings from being worn. This type of point is usually similar in size to the Clovis Points and has been found in and associated with the remains of extinct bison and date a little more recent than Folsom Points.

**Projectile point** – Typically a bifacially flaked implement with a pointed tip and sharp sides with a base of various styles that is meant to penetrate animal hide causing a fatal wound for the purpose of retrieving game for food or protection and can be made from bone, ivory or fire hardened wood and attached to a spear, dart or foreshaft and in post Archaic times the tip of an arrow shot with a bow.

**Solutrean** – A culture that existed between 21,000 and 17,000 years ago in the Iberian Peninsula region of western Europe including southern France, Spain and Portugal that has been postulated to have migrated by boat along the glacial ice reaching into the north Atlantic entering northeastern North America with a big blade technology that has become the proposed source of the Clovis culture.

**Teleportation** – The theoretical transfer of matter from one point to another without traversing the physical space between the two places and can include different time intervals.

**Younger Dryas** – A geological and climatological period from 12,900 to 11,700 years ago which saw a sharp decline in temperature and moisture over most of the northern hemisphere at the end of the Pleistocene epoch and the beginning of the Holocene period. Changes appear to have been influenced by longitude and altitude with variations in isolated regions still being correlated.

**"The First American"**
Sculpture by Curtis Fort, Tatum, New Mexico